Eroticizing Discipline

Dominance, Submission and Exquisite Pleasure

H. Hargrove

CCB Publishing
British Columbia, Canada

Eroticizing Discipline:
Dominance, Submission and Exquisite Pleasure

Copyright ©2012 by H. Hargrove
ISBN-13   978-1-77143-019-7
First Edition

Library and Archives Canada Cataloguing in Publication
Hargrove, H.
Eroticizing discipline : dominance, submission and exquisite pleasure /
written by H. Hargrove.
ISBN 978-1-77143-019-7
Also available in electronic format.
Additional cataloguing data available from Library and Archives Canada

Cover design by the author.

Publisher: CCB Publishing
             British Columbia, Canada
             www.ccbpublishing.com

Preface

The phenomenal success of *Fifty Shades of Grey* has illuminated the sublime pleasure many associate with erotic discipline. Of all the options inside the infamous red room, Anna came to accept that the thought of being spanked was one of her favorite turn-ons.

Many individuals drawn to literature depicting this kink fixate on the rituals associated with traditional corporal punishment and the roles they play in its erotic component. But many works in this genre concentrate on actual discipline, and pay only lip service to these rituals and their often critical link in the development of an erotic component.

Each story in this collection is rooted in these rituals of traditional discipline, while relating in depth the sexual arousal and heighted pleasure that are so interrelated for devotees. *Eroticizing Discipline* depicts cases of an erotic component developing from an association with an aspect of corporal punishment, evolving, and becoming an integral part of that individual's sexuality.

Contents

Disciplining Sheila

This is written with Sheila's consent. She will, on occasion, contribute her own words.

For the past two years I have been with an extraordinarily beautiful and wonderful lady. From the fourth week of our relationship, erotic discipline has played a major role. During the second month we discovered a possible link that might cause Sheila, a woman who had never been spanked as an adult, to nervously crave the punishment she desperately needs. What I will provide you is a glimpse into our lives, the loving but stern discipline that is such a key to the success of our relationship, and the numerous, intimate, late-night conversations in which Sheila has revealed the details of the possible link - the punishments that controlled and molded her through her childhood and teen years.

I met Sheila through a friend at a bar. Late at night. Long odds for a relationship. Her stunning beauty was mesmerizing - classic, high cheekbones, perfectly sculpted chin, small, neat, aquiline features, blond hair pulled back like the Duchess of Kent. A Heidi Klum look-alike, although shorter. She wore a short, dark business suit that showed off her muscular calves, beautifully tapered legs, and gave a hint of the fullness of her breasts. When she turned to walk to the restroom I saw that her hips and bottom were smaller than I was accustomed to, but her tight, round little ass soon became an object of my worship.

Sheila is extremely bright, but displays the character-istics that are the basis of "blond jokes". Unorganized, forgetful, messy, tardy, more than a bit spoiled, with a penchant for emotional outbursts - particularly after three, rather than two, glasses of Chardonnay. Of course, for every negative there are three positives.

By the third week we were spending a great deal of time together, and discovered many shared interests and passions. We both loved to dance, play tennis, work out, read, listen to music, cook, travel, and have long, intense conversations about anything and everything – our gazes rarely leaving the other. Both of us are serious romantics. And from the beginning, the sex was playful, imaginative, and terrific. I determined early on that Sheila was perhaps the most sexual person I had ever been around, male or female...but without knowing it.

But her chronic tardiness was a nuisance. After she showed up late once again I remarked in an offhand manner, "I might have to give you a good spanking the next time you're late."

It was on my second or third threat that she gave me a look that meant something. I wasn't sure what.

We were in her living room when I decided to follow through. I don't remember the exact circumstances, but we were next to each other on the couch, she had misbehaved, and I told her I was going to give her a spanking. Looking at me she said, "No" - but not very convincingly. I told her to lie across my lap and she stared at me. When I pulled her arm toward me she didn't resist, and let me turn her over. She had on a short skirt, which I pulled up over her

2

waist, and sheer, high cut nylon panties, which I pushed down to her knees. She shivered noticeably. Although in her later thirties, Sheila has the body of a woman years younger.

From that first time, there has always been a wave of fascination and desire that runs through me when I expose the creamy skin of her beautiful, tight little ass, get a glimpse of the tiny, pink, puckered opening only partially hidden between her firm cheeks, and the thatch of hair and pink folds just above the smooth, muscular loveliness of her thighs.

Something told me to spank her fairly soundly that first time.

After a few minutes she started reaching back and trying to cover her behind with her hands, half-heartedly it seemed to me - but she never asked me to stop. I remember telling her, "This is what you will get every time you misbehave. And I sense you are going to misbehave a lot." When I finished, I talked softly about her need for discipline as I gently caressed her pink, warm bottom. She panted audibly. The sex that followed was phenomenal. Slow, delicious, wild, wanton - with both of us all over the other's body. An hour, two hours - it's never fast. It's always furious.

It was a week or so later when I sent her into the back yard to get a switch, then ordered her into the bathroom to wait for me. After leaving her alone for a good ten minutes, I walked in and told her that what I was about to do could be expected every time she has one of her little "going crazy moments." A few too many glasses of wine after dinner and a political argument that turned into personal insults was the reason I was now ordering her to bend over and grab her ankles. She only had on running tights, which I pulled down until they were bunched at her feet. The view of her gorgeous, tanned legs and white bottom, arched over so that the hair between her thighs and folds peeked out - made it very hard to concentrate on my primary responsibility of giving Sheila a switching she would remember. Regaining my composure, I managed to use the switch on her bottom until she was squirming, but also panting lightly. She never asked me to stop. After I finished she immediately turned, went to her knees, frantically pulled my zipper down, pulled my dick out, and took it deep into her mouth. She was incredibly skilled, and wouldn't release me from the warm, wet paradise of her mouth until I exploded.

Later that evening, snuggled up very close to each other in bed, we had the first of what would become a ritual for us - long, intimate, open conversations about Sheila, me, sometimes discipline, and sex. She said in a whisper, "When you pull my panties down to spank me, or make me take them down - it drives me crazy. I'm nervous, but God I'm turned on." And then later, "It wasn't the first time, you know. The only time in my life I've ever been really good was when I knew my crazy mother would go nuts if she thought I messed up. I got yelled at and punished all the time. Sylvia told me she'd send us to get a switch. I guess I managed to forget some of the details."

"When did Sylvia tell you that?"

"I asked her. I was curious after you started giving me spankings."

"Did you tell Sylvia how I discipline you?"

"Sylvia? God no! She's really straight. Don't ever tell

her. Some people…I mean…it would probably turn me on if they knew. But then I'm finding out that everything turns me on. But not Sylvia."

"Tell me more about your Mom spanking you." I slowly pressed my hard dick between the cheeks of her ass, spooning up closer and slipping my hand between her breasts.

"I hated it…what I remember. Then sometimes she would tell me that Dad was going to wear me out when he got home."

"Did he?"

"Yeah…sometimes."

"Did it turn you on at all?" I asked.

"I don't think so, no. I never thought about it like that. I used to dread it, but it was kind of weird. I need to think about that."

My fingers found the slick lips of her pussy and after a few moments I slowly replaced them by pushing my steel hard dick deep into her…to return the pleasure she had so unselfishly given me earlier.

One of the troublesome issues Sheila and I have is my ex-wife's family. I was married for twenty years, and had a sixteen-year-old daughter when Sheila and I met. My ex has a large family, most of them live locally, and over the years I had grown very close to some of her siblings and her parents. And, of course, they are still my daughter's family. I enjoy seeing them on occasion, and there have been numerous events that my daughter has been involved in that my ex and members of her family have attended. Sheila has never understood why I still need to see them.

Much of her attitude originates from her lack of a cohesive family, and then there's her severe insecurity. Funny - how extreme beauty often exacerbates that condition. I always try to be sensitive to her feelings. But at times it becomes too much to take.

I was working in my home office one afternoon when she came in and immediately attacked me for accepting an invitation for us to go to my ex's to celebrate an award our daughter had won. It was at least the third time this particular gathering had been hotly debated. I listened patiently for a few minutes and explained, again, that it was important to my daughter that I be there. When the anger in her voice rose dramatically, I spoke slowly, but forcefully, "Watch out, you're about to get in trouble." She ignored me, and continued to rant and rave.

"All right, Sheila. I'm too busy trying to finish this contract to deal with you now, and we have to meet Terry at 7:30 for dinner. But some time tomorrow I'm going to take my belt off - and I think you know what that means." By now I was used to it - the shudder and slight shake that runs through her body when I tell her she is going to be disciplined.

"No. I don't want a spanking."

There is always this dilemma for me when Sheila truly needs to be disciplined. Looking at her - the innocent, little girl beauty and pleading look, and realizing that she knows she's going to get a sound spanking - it's hard for me to focus only on punishing her properly.

"Then don't ever start on me again about Laura's family. Because every time you do, I'm going to tan your behind."

It was 6:30 the next evening when I heard the car door shut in the driveway. Sheila walked in with salads and sushi, kissed me, and stepped into the kitchen. "God, I'm hungry as a horse. I'm going to have a glass of wine. Want a beer?"

"I have some unfinished business with you - before we have a drink."

Sheila looked up in time to see me unbuckle the leather belt and pull it slowly out of my jeans, then double it.

"Bob, no. I don't want a spanking," she said, as the very visible shudder shook her body.

"Get in the bedroom. Right now." There was a tone to my voice she had learned to obey, and she didn't say a word as she walked by me. I followed, watching the muscles of her beautiful, tanned legs flex beneath the short hem of the pale blue sundress.

I pulled one of the large decorative pillows into the middle of the bed. "Lay on your stomach, with the pillow under your hips." She did as she was told. I reached over, pulled her dress up over her waist, then pulled her sheer, blue panties down to her ankles. She still had on her heeled sandals, and when I stepped back the scene was well past alluring. The pillow arched her bottom just enough so that the patch of dark blond hair and the pink, glistening lips of her pussy were perfectly framed between her tanned thighs and creamy buttocks, and the puckered, hairless bud of her anus was clearly visible.

She began to pant. For a moment I wanted to drop the belt and bury my tongue between those perfect cheeks and thighs. But I knew she needed this, and there would be time later.

"You may not be able to sit down for dinner after I finish with you. Are you going to drop this nonsense about my ex-family?"

"I don't know."

"I bet you'll know in a minute." Her first, brief orgasm came as I pulled the tip of the belt lightly up over her thighs, across the thatch of hair, up between the cheeks of her ass, then said, "You're about to get a spanking you won't forget for a while." My arm rose and fell slowly at first, but within a few minutes her bottom was a bright pink. Then she was trying to squirm out of the way, raising and lowering her hips, reaching back to cover her behind with her hands.

"Are you going to stop bringing it up?"

I knew she could never do anything more than say "yes." It isn't in Sheila's nature to ever admit she's wrong. Even when we both know she is.

Finally she said "Yes", and it was my cue to use the belt a little harder.

"Are you sure?"

"Yes."

I can never be harsh with Sheila; I care for her too much. But we both agree that when she misbehaves she needs to be soundly spanked, and since this was the first time I used the belt, I wanted to be sure to leave an impression. Many couples play with the real discipline, erotic discipline issue, but with us it really works. Particularly when she throws one of her tantrums. No amount of reasoning or talking can calm her down. She always initially resists being spanked when she's upset, but at some point during the spanking she calms down, accepts it, making up is automatic, and we have white-hot sex.

Days of anger, distance and silence are avoided. We quickly return to a state of happiness and contentment.

"OK. It's over now. I hope you've learned a lesson." As I spoke gently to her, I lightly stroked the pink, hot cheeks of her bottom. My tongue then started across the smooth flesh, completely coating one cheek with a warm film, then the other. As it slipped down between the tight, round little buttocks and began to flick at her lovely little anus, my fingers slowly caressed the smooth skin between her thighs, moved higher, then brushed along the lips of her pussy. My tongue was tickling electric pleasure into the bundles of receptive nerves around her anus at the same time I slipped two of my fingers into her pussy. Sheila was moaning loudly. I reached my left hand under her dress, pushed her bra over her breasts, and began to twirl her nipples between my fingers. Cupping one breast in my hand, I massaged it, then returned to her erect nipple. I continued to probe her ass and pussy - slowly, then faster, then slowly again. I changed positions, slid my tongue down between her legs, found her clit, then gently pushed a wet finger up into her ass. Even when I stopped to get my breath, my fingers were moving, circling, probing, caressing. As always happens, when I have both hands and my tongue working in concert, a strong shudder shook her body.

After many minutes of slow, exquisite pleasure, as if on cue, we were both up, tearing each other's clothes off. Sheila pushed me back on the bed, put one hand on the shaft of my throbbing dick, the other on my balls, then stared as if they were her most prized possessions as she began fondling me. She slipped a finger first into her pussy, then into my ass, and took my dick deep inside her mouth. I lay back, groaned. Ecstasy. I tried to relax and revel in the incredible feel of her strong but gentle sucking motion, her fingers expertly caressing first my balls, then my ass, then my balls again. She would continue until I erupted in her mouth, or needed to be inside her. That time came.

Within seconds she was on her hands and knees and I was pushing deep inside her warm wetness. I drove into her, hard at first, then gently, then hard again, over and over.

God, it was exquisite. Amazing. As always. Finally, after one more shudder and cry from her, I exploded.

Once our breath returned we kissed, long and gently, then dozed in each other arms. The wine, beer and sushi had to wait. Dinner was at 11:00 p.m.

The next night we were in bed, spooned close, when I asked, "Was your bottom sore today?"

"Not really. Well, maybe a little. Makes me remember," she said with a sly smile.

I could feel my dick thickening, pressing between the cheeks of her ass. "You needed it, you know. I mean the belt." My voice was soft, smooth, almost a monotone. "And something else. About a week ago you said something bitchy, the same old family thing, when we were at Donna's. Do you want to guess what will happen if you do that again?"

"Will you spank me? There?"

"Absolutely."

"In front of her…or them?"

"I might. Or at least take you into the bathroom. They'll damn sure know." Her body trembled slightly.

"It made me think," she said.

"What made you think," I said.

"When you took your belt off."

"What did you think about?"

"My Dad."

"Yes? What about your Dad?"

"He used a belt when he spanked me."

"Will you tell me about it?"

"What do you want to know?"

"How old were you when he gave you your last spanking?"

"I'm not sure. High school. Fifteen, maybe sixteen."

"Tell me about the last time."

"I don't remember too much. I mean about which time was the last."

"Then how do you know how old you were?"

"There were a couple of times when guys brought me home. After going out. I was at least fifteen."

"What would happen? Tell me exactly what would happen."

"Dad was gone a lot. In the military. He wasn't around too much. A lot of times Mom would tell him if I was bad."

"Were you really bad?"

"No. I was really good. The only time in my life. Because I was afraid. But Mom was crazy. A wild crazy woman when she drank. An alcoholic. To her, everything I did was bad."

"So what would she do?"

"Sometimes, after she yelled at me and called me names...she'd tell me Dad was going to wear me out when he got home."

"And would he?" I slowly slipped my dick into Sheila's pussy from behind, pushing gently, as I kept questioning her. She pressed her hips back against me, until I was all the way in.

We were so close, wrapped tightly in each other's arms, discussing things so intimate, making very slow, very wonderful love.

"Yeah. Sometimes."

"And were you afraid when you knew he was going to spank you?"

"I hated it. Waiting."

"What would he do? Tell me everything."

"He'd make me go to my room. He kept the belt in his drawer. He'd get it or sometimes he'd make me go and get it."

"Did you have a room of your own."

"No. I shared it with Sylvia."

"Was she ever in there when he spanked you?"

"One time...maybe...I think. But not usually. I don't

remember too much."

"Go on."

"He'd make me take off my dress, or jeans."

"All your clothes?"

"No. Just my dress or jeans, and my panties."

"He'd make you take them off?"

"He'd make me pull them down."

"Then what?"

"He'd make me bend over the bed. Or lay across it."

"Bend over? How?"

"With my hands on the bed."

"Did it hurt?"

"Yes. He spanked me pretty hard. Not brutal…not really abusive. I mean, a lot of kids got spanked back then. Pretty common."

"You told me before it didn't turn you on. Are you sure?"

"No. I definitely never thought it did. But now that I've been thinking back - I mean, it turns me on so much when you do it, even though I'm nervous, and in a way don't want you to do it. I think there may have been something, some feeling I can't describe or put my finger on. The memories are vague. My childhood wasn't good. I couldn't wait to leave, and I'm sure I've suppressed a lot of it. But there may have been something other than my fear, the embarrassment, the sting. Maybe there was some strange, imperceptible attraction. It was about the only attention he ever gave me, and I'm sure that's a key. He didn't really seem like a father. He was gone so much. He was a very distant, cold man."

I kept rocking gently inside Sheila's pussy, slowly, cupping her breasts in my hand, caressing her nipples, as we continued to talk. It was silky smooth, almost dreamlike, an incredible turn-on - listening, sharing, fantasizing, while I was connected to her, filling her, seemingly a part of her.

"Can you try to remember that last time…that he spanked you."

"It's hard to remember which time. I know I came home late a couple of times after a date and got in trouble. There was another time that I wasn't late, but my Mom came out and threw one of her tantrums. Called me a slut. Screamed and yelled. I was just sitting in the car with a guy in the driveway. Talking. Doing nothing wrong."

"Did she punish you after you came in the house? Did she spank you?"

"I just don't remember. Sometimes she did. I was so upset. But I do remember coming in late one night and my Dad was home. I came in the door and he was standing there and I knew what was going to happen."

"What did happen?"

"His eyes. They were so dark. And hard. He glared at me. And he already had the belt in his hand."

"Go on."

"I'll tell you what I can remember. He told me to go upstairs and then followed me up. He lectured me for a minute or so. He never said much. Then he made me take off my jeans. I had to lie across the bed on my stomach and then he pulled my panties down. He spanked me for a long time. I'm not sure if it was that time…but one time I just lay there for a long time after he finished and left my room."

My dick was rock hard. As I increased the intensity of the rocking motion…and the thrusts…Sheila began to moan. I felt her shudder. Usually I could last as long as I wanted to…and I usually wanted to drag out the pleasure. But that night…I exploded quickly. God she turned me on.

I don't know what to say. You said it all. You write really well. OK, the sex is amazing. Wonderful. You do so many things to me that no one else has done. I love it. And when you make me do things. That's what I love the most. Promise you'll always make me do things. Make me do everything.

I know you want me to talk about the spankings. When you tell me you're going to spank me it drives me crazy. And when you pull my panties down before you do it, it makes me even crazier, if that's possible. God it turns me on. I don't know if it's linked in some way to the spankings I got at home …those times when I was a teenager. Maybe. But I just don't know.

Sheila

Remembering

Down to just about one passion that's working. Can't see too well...can't read much. Can't hear much either... which is a blessing with chattering, blathering nurses. Head still swims like I'm drunk. My juices haven't flowed full speed since the damned accident. But that shudder and hint of warmth I feel in my loins is comforting. And my memory is still a steel trap. Eyes closed, head back against my pillow. If I'm not interrupted...maybe I can start my afternoon off right.

After many years the image remains crystal clear. I was sitting in the living room of the large, elegant brownstone on Lyme Street in Boston. Beacon Hill. Prestigious neighborhood. Mr. Johnstone walked in...tall, ramrod straight posture, distinguished, full head of silver hair, perfectly attired in a charcoal gray, double breasted suit and blue tie. He possessed the angular, fine features of a patrician, which he was. I was twenty two, and in these surroundings, in the presence of this man...I was impressed.

The interview didn't last long. There were the standard questions in Mr. Johnstone's impeccable, formal British brogue, about my prior employment and method of managing the cleaning and general upkeep of a residence of this size and quality. My work ethic? Could I accept the fact that I would be rewarded for being efficient and resourceful? And disciplined for errors of judgment, carelessness, and neglect? Whoa! My first clue, but his line of questioning quickly moved elsewhere after I instinctively nodded and murmured "yes".

It would be my second job as a housekeeper after becoming disenchanted with secretarial school, and my experience and enthusiasm must have hit the right chord, because he handed me an employment agreement, told me to look it over and sign and bring it to his office if it met my approval.

The pay was excellent. I would have quarters, a room of my own, and based on the size of the living room and rich furnishings I assumed I would be significantly elevating my standard of living. I would be the only housekeeper and have both responsibility and leeway to make decisions. There was a section of the agreement which dealt with acceptable standards of work, attention to detail, the requirement of obeying orders or directions from both Mr. and Mrs. Johnstone, and treating them with respect and reverence for their position. *Position* was never clearly defined, but in addition to being the Lord and Lady of this very fine house, they were apparently also a Lord and Lady in some official capacity, as members of the gentry in their native land.

There was a short, two sentence paragraph stating something like *initiative, efficiency and exemplary completion of assigned duties will be rewarded with either cash bonuses and/or compensatory time off. Neglect of duties, failure to meet required standards in all tasks, and any signs of disrespect will result in discipline, which, if warranted, will take the form of a reasonable application of corporal punishment.*

Well...there it was. I had a choice. I looked around, read the agreement again, felt a twinge of fear...the slightest tingle of something else...apprehension, maybe? I wasn't sure...and signed it.

When I walked into the study, directly off the living room, to return the signed agreement to Mr. Johnstone, Mrs. Johnstone was standing by his desk. She was also tall, stunningly beautiful for a woman who looked to be in her forties, with a trim figure, perfect, fine, sculpted facial features, and a bun arrangement of thick, blond hair. She nodded and offered a faint, regal smile when Mr. Johnstone introduced me. I was aware of her eyes never leaving me as I accepted the position and handed the agreement to her husband.

I was told to report the following Monday, with my bags, ready to move in and begin work. I was then shown the door.

It was at least two weeks, during which time I earned an afternoon and evening off, along with a crisp twenty dollar bill for my exemplary work and attitude, before Mr. Johnstone confronted me with a problem. I don't remember the exact problem...just the result. I was told to report to his study after I had finished cleaning from the evening meal.

Concentrating was difficult for the rest of the day. But I didn't want to make matters worse. Thinking back, it's difficult to separate my thoughts then from what I know and feel now. There was certainly some fear...and a good dose of anxiety...and again a hint of something else.

The ritual never varied from that first time. I walked in at the appointed time and found Mr. Johnstone sitting at his desk. He described the problem, then told me he was going to discipline me. He stood to his full, erect height and regal bearing, opened his desk drawer and took out a brown leather belt without a buckle, then told me to bend across his desk and raise my skirt. I had been issued three uniforms when I arrived for work that first day. Short, light blue skirts and blue and white blouses. A fairly standard, but classy, housekeeper outfit.

I remember thinking I should protest...refuse...but I stayed silent and obeyed. I was uncomfortable...but not *only* scared. Something else. Confused feelings.

My mother spanked me. I didn't like it, but I didn't dread it. Mainly a nuisance. She loved me too much for it to really hurt. I'd have to go across her knee, or for serious misbehavior I was sent to fetch a switch from the backyard willow tree.

Mom remarried when I was twelve. The last time she spanked me I was fourteen, and a bolt of panic shot through me when she announced my punishment in front of Frankie. Was he going to watch? When I was ordered to my room he didn't follow, but after she finished and I glanced at my red bottom in the mirror, I thought of him again and felt a tiny shudder. There would be thousands of those shudders throughout the rest of my life. Many not so tiny. My body and thoughts had been changing rapidly. Frankie was Italian, dark, handsome, really built, with a full head of wavy black hair, and five years younger than Mom. He was hot. The thought that he could have watched... seen my bare bottom arched and squirming over her lap... or even spanked me himself. An early...confusing image... and feelings.

Mr. Johnstone was very formal and reserved, with slow, measured movements as he walked around the desk and stood in back of me as I was bent forward over the massive, hand carved, antique desk. I raised my skirt and held it above my waist...then waited. For a few moments nothing happened, then I felt his fingers slip under the waistband of my panties and lower them to just above my knees. Now, suddenly, I felt panic...and something else. I was bent forward, my bare bottom and likely my pubic hair and lips of my pussy in clear view of a very handsome, distinguished gentleman...and he was going to spank me. I still remember that moment I realized the *something else* feeling was sexual arousal. And the almost instantaneous thought of confusion that flashed through my mind.

The spanking hurt. But not that much. After the first couple of blows and the initial sting - I was fairly certain I was safe. Then I felt the first hint of warmth. Before he was finished I pressed my legs tightly together so he couldn't see the wetness I felt between my thighs. Later, in my room, lying in bed, my mind raced with contradictory thoughts and feelings as I relived my punishment. My hand slipped under the waistband of my pajamas and I again felt the wetness I had sensed while being punished. Within seconds of finding the tiny knob of my clitoris with my finger I exploded with a rush of ecstasy.

After lying very still...with my eyes closed...I realized I wasn't ready to sleep. Again my fingers slipped inside my waistband. My other hand found the nipple of my breast. I was quickly wet again. It took a bit longer the second time. I pulled my knees toward my chest and spread my legs. The convulsions were almost as strong... and they lasted longer. I went to sleep confused...but content.

BJ was the house chef, and the only other full time house employee. He was an Indian boy from New Delhi, a couple of years older than me, and very handsome with his dark skin and eyes, narrow, angular face, and slender, muscular build. He was a very accomplished cricket player, and spent his off hours in Cambridge competing with Harvard and MIT students with a similar love and passion for the game. The Johnstones had spent a good deal of time in India, loved the food, and hired BJ from a local restaurant.

I was hesitant to discuss the discipline I was receiving on what seemed like a fairly regular basis, but I was also curious about what BJ knew or experienced. There was, I perceived, an attraction or connection of some sort between us from the first day I was at the house, but we initially kept our distance and were formal in our interaction. Then one day I blurted it out. "When you mess up do you get disciplined?"

"What do you mean, Irene?" His English was impeccable.

I gave him a quick version of what happened in Mr. Johnstone's study and although he listened quietly, I could sense more than a polite interest in what I was telling him. He was about to speak when the phone rang and he began a long conversation. I thought it was best that I leave.

I had been at the Johnstone house a couple of months when I was told to report to the study after dinner for failing to promptly pick up an order of dry cleaning. An important jacket that Mr. Johnstone wanted for an event wasn't available to him. As I entered the study Mrs.

Johnstone, standing just inside the door, offered me a slight, tight smile.

After Mr. Johnstone disciplined me the first time, and my hours of bedtime pleasure, I realized that the discomfort was more than compensated for by the pleasure. Or was the discomfort a necessary ingredient for that heightened level of pleasure? I hadn't sorted it all out...and to this day...lying in this bed years later...still haven't. But I now know enough to realize that for me there was always that delicious mix of anxiety, apprehension, having something done to me that I don't really want...or maybe really do... being forced...ordered...being exposed...vulnerable...and *punished*.

Now, with the presence of Mrs. Johnstone, there was an interruption of the apprehension and warmth I had come to expect. Serious confusion of thoughts and feelings. My mind raced...between the moment and what was coming.

Mr. Johnstone's lecture was familiar, though being without his favorite jacket at an important function seemed to raise his level of irritation beyond what he normally displayed. When he stood and took the belt from the drawer I was very aware that Mrs. Johnstone had not moved an inch. "Bend forward over the desk and pull up your skirt, Irene."

I was nervous. Beyond warm apprehension. I hesitated for a moment, then moved to the edge of the desk. I sensed Mrs. Johnstone taking a step forward. I pulled up my dress, and, as I remember it now, Mr. Johnstone was even more deliberate...even slower with his movements...as he pulled my panties down, this time to my ankles. I knew goose bumps covered my flesh as soon as the cool air touched every crevice and opening…and I shuddered slightly. There was a long pause…longer than before I believe…before I felt the belt sting my bottom.

I don't know if it took longer with Mrs. Johnstone there…but my pussy still got wet. I had stopped holding my legs together during my punishments, as I hoped Mr. Johnstone's hand might end up between them after he finished spanking me. It never had. On this occasion I did press my thighs together because I surely didn't want her to notice.

"Darling, I'm not sure your spanking is having the proper affect. We surely wouldn't want it to give Irene any comfort. Spread you legs, Irene." I hesitated. "Now." Her tone was very firm. "You don't want me to have to punish you."

I quickly spread my legs apart. I knew. And I knew she knew. Mrs. Johnstone moved closer…until she was directly in back of me…only a few feet away. The spanking resumed and lasted longer than the others I had received. As soon as Mr. Johnstone laid the belt on the desk, she said, "I want you to check her, Darling."

I felt fingers slide up the inside of my thigh and along the lips of my now-dripping pussy. "She's very wet, isn't she?"

"Yes," Mr. Johnstone answered his wife, "she's very wet."

His fingers slid into me, lingered, gently probed, found my clit, then moved slowly up between my cheeks until they brushed across my anus. I was fighting not to orgasm. His caresses continued. I couldn't help myself, spread my legs further apart, and arched my bottom higher. His fingers went back deep inside me while his other hand slid slowly between my cheeks. Suddenly he stepped back. There was a long silence. I stayed very still, bent forward, my legs spread, my glistening pussy and bottom on full display.

"We'll have to decide how to handle this situation, Darling," she said as she walked out of the room.

"Very well, Irene. You can put yourself back together now."

God, how I wanted him to stay.

I was too turned on to accept bringing myself to orgasm, so I headed to the kitchen to find BJ, with the excuse of looking for desert if I needed it. He was putting away groceries.

"Damn, I just got it again." He looked puzzled. "You know, disciplined."

He pulled out a chair from the desk, sat down, and asked, "Please tell me exactly what happened."

I began describing what happened...starting with Mr. Johnstone's order that I report to the study for neglecting to pick up the laundry. Before I mentioned Mrs. Johnstone's appearance I related what I had come to expect...told him in detail what had happened the first three or four times I had been spanked. He constantly interrupted me. Asked me to repeat certain descriptions. Suddenly he stood up, moved forward and embraced me. His lips were all over mine and his tongue slid into my mouth.

Within a few frantic moments we were in the large pantry and he was on his knees pulling my panties down.

He slid his hand up under my blouse and bra, across my breast; then, still on his knees, held my skirt up with his other hand, put his mouth over my pussy and started licking me. I was pinned against jars of tomatoes, but it was intense, explosive pleasure. His fingers and tongue seemed to be all over me at once, and a warm wetness teased, then entered me in more than one place.

After a few minutes of gasping ecstasy, BJ stood up, quickly removed my clothes, pulled his pants and undershorts down to reveal a beautiful, large, dark, swollen cock, turned me around, and plunged deep into me from behind. We managed to cum almost in unison.

It was a few days later, at night, again in the kitchen, and this time we were having dessert. BJ brought it up. "Has Mrs. Johnstone ever had anything to do with disciplining you?"

"Well," I said with a wink, "you didn't let me finish my story the other night. It was the only time, but she watched."

"She only watched?"

"She said a few things."

"Well, I have a story for you. But first, tell me what she said."

"No, you owe me a story. You go first."

"Mrs. Johnstone interviewed me, and she gave me an agreement that sounds like yours. I questioned her about the discipline and corporal punishment part and she looked right into my eyes for a moment, then said, "I'm the one who will discipline you, BJ. Don't you think you can handle it?" I was stunned, but I sure wasn't going to say I

25

couldn't."

"Nothing happened for about a week. And then I forgot about a request Mrs. Johnstone had for an evening meal. She came into the kitchen after dinner, said she didn't ever want it to happen again, and told me to come to the study after I finished putting everything away."

"Sounds like similar scenarios, except she was standing, waiting for me, and holding the belt in her hand. She immediately told me to take off my jeans. I took them off. Then she told me to step over to the front of the desk and bend over it with my chest flat across the top. I hesitated. She was very stern, said something like "Now, BJ. Do as I tell you." I bent across the desk. Nothing happened for a minute, then I felt her fingers under the waistband of my underpants and she slid them down to my ankles. She told me to spread my legs. Man, was I exposed. She said she was going to give me a good whipping, and I'd get the same every time I didn't obey her or follow her orders."

The shudder came suddenly as my mind's eye pictured BJ bent over the desk, his tight, muscular ass arched up and his beautiful cock hanging down and clearly visible between his spread legs.

"She really spanked me hard. I tried not to squirm but it was tough. She stopped for a minute and I wasn't sure she was finished, but then I felt her hand wrap around my dick. Man...I was hard as a rock." He paused.

"And then?"

"BJ, come here, please." Mrs. Johnstone's voice cut through the kitchen and BJ was quickly up and through the door.

I figured BJ would knock on my door later that night, and he did. As he slid my pajama bottoms off I asked him to finish his story. Instead of speaking, his mouth went immediately to my thigh, his tongue licked at me, then moved up to find my already dripping pussy lips. After a long session with his tongue sliding up and down my lips and over my clit, he gently rolled me over. His fingers now caressed my pussy, while his tongue started darting between the cheeks of my bottom and lightly flicking across my anus. The fingers of his other hand played with my breasts. I was on fire.

I remember marveling at how skilled and experienced a lover BJ was. From our conversations I believed that he was not actively practicing a religion, but he was born a Hindu, and I would have thought exposure at a young age to that culture might inhibit sexuality. I was employed by the Johnstones for less than a year, but my sexual education moved at warp speed during those months, and my addiction to the amazing intensity of pleasure inherent in an erotic component to discipline was cemented forever.

I was exhausted after the multiple hours of sexual pleasure BJ and I exchanged that evening. I did my best to reciprocate each caress…to each body part. But as I lay in bed I thought that perhaps I still had not had enough. Images were dancing in my mind of Mrs. Johnstone, with her perfectly coiffed blond bun, in her perfectly tailored, exquisite suit, reaching between BJ's legs as he bent forward across the desk, wrapping his balls and huge erection in the palm of her hand, and squeezing and caressing them until his cum splashed onto the floor…or filling her mouth while she knelt under him…or filling her pussy as she bent over the desk, her skirt pulled up and her panties around her ankles. I vowed to ask BJ what *really* happened.

It was a couple of days later when I found the time to raise the question again. He smiled, then said, "Okay, but I'm still waiting to hear what she said while she watched Mr. Johnstone spank you. Where did I stop?"

"You were bent over the desk, she had just spanked you and she reached between your legs and put her hand around your cock."

"Yeah. I almost exploded right then. But I managed to wait. She turned me around, then went down on her knees and started sucking on me. Man, was it hard not to cum. But she seemed to know when to stop."

"She got up and went over to the couch, then told me to come and undress her...slowly. I remember the *slowly* part. I took all of her clothes off. She has a very nice body for a woman her age. As soon as I pulled her panties off she grabbed my head and pulled it down to her pussy. I knew what to do. I was really getting into licking her when she pushed me away, turned around and bent over the arm of the sofa. She spread the cheeks of her ass and said, "Now I want you to lick me here."

"She was really getting hot...moaning and groaning while I was sliding my tongue across her ass."

"I want you to fuck me now! That's what she told me. She was panting...gasping. "In my pussy," she said. But if you don't do it well I'll spank you again...harder...then make you fuck me in my ass."

"Man, that got me going. I don't think I have to tell

you what happened next. Okay, now it's your turn. What did she say?"

Sealing the Deal

My earliest memories? Going with Dad to buy the new, 1950, green Chevy coupe when I was five. And likely a year or two earlier, lying in what I think was a large, crib-like bed, playing with my penis.

Spanking turned me on from an early age; about six or seven the best I can remember, when the neighbor girl first told me her mother gave her a spanking with a hairbrush. At that young age I was an adept enough at interrogation to quickly learn that she was marched in to her bedroom where her mom ordered her to lay across her lap, then pulled down her panties and gave her a paddling. Her bare bottom, arched, waiting...an enduring image. There were other punishments to hear about, and a little later read about, and I was an avid student. I also was fascinated with doctor's visits and examinations, and on more than one occasion I talked my girl playmates into undressing so I could examine them, concentrating most of my attention on a close inspection of their bottoms. But anything that conjured an image of a spanking was like a drug to me. Not yet knowing anything about the actual sex act, what I did know was that whenever I heard, read or saw anything related to a spanking, or just imagined it – I got a fuzzy, warm feeling flowing through my body and a hard penis. By the time I was in my mid-teen years, I was spending hours in the library investigating and reading about corporal punishment and its historical connection to eroticism, particularly in the homes, schools and convents of the British Isles and the U.S. But that day when I was fifteen, entering my third year of high school, and spending the afternoon at Joe McFarland's house - sealed my fetish for a lifetime.

Joe and I were classmates and neighbors. I spent many an afternoon at his house, listening to the latest 45's and searching through his father's girlie magazine collection – when we thought his mom was a safe distance away.

Ah, yes, Mrs. McFarland. It was my first experience, but not my last, with a neurotic woman who drinks too much. On top of that - she was a flaming redhead. When the weather was warm, she walked around the house in tiny shorts, which often didn't quite cover the cheeks of her ass above her long, shapely, freckle-covered legs. If she bent the right way, or got up the right way – I could catch a glimpse of red pubic hair. No panties for Mrs. McFarland. She was a frazzled, frantic woman, often smelled of alcohol, and it seemed as if threatening her children was at least half of what came out of her mouth.

Joe's sister Connie was a year younger and about to start her second year at our school. She was maturing quickly, and her breasts and bottom jiggled enticingly enough to make me always want to look. She was also a redhead, but seemed to be growing into a more rounded, voluptuous shape than her mom's.

"Do you want me to take you into the bathroom? I'm about to get the belt. Don't make me tan your behind." These were all common threats to both Joe and Connie that Mrs. McFarland screamed on a regular basis while I was at their house. I was sent home once because Joe was going to get a whipping, but many of the threats remained only threats.

I was at their house one afternoon when I heard Connie ordered into the bathroom after some yelling and threats, and I fantasized about it for weeks. I asked Joe for as many details of their punishments as I could without raising suspicion, and replayed over and over Mrs. McFarland's order, Connie's protestations, and then the slam of the door. There were other sounds, muffled from Joe's upstairs room, but there was no doubt Connie was getting a spanking.

A month or so went by until another afternoon when we were in Joe's room listening to music and heard his mom start yelling at Connie, then threatening her. I sat up and began listening and Joe shot me a quick smile. What came next was loud enough to be heard very clearly. "I'm going to get the belt, young lady. Get in the bathroom right now...right now!"

Joe motioned for me to follow him. We crept down the staircase and waited until we heard the door slam, then he darted out the front door and I followed. We reached the back yard and tiptoed, hunched over, to the small window. He motioned for me to look, I slowly lifted my head, and through the open slats of the blinds I saw Connie bent over with her hands on her ankles, her dress up over her waist, and Mrs. McFarland lowering her panties to her knees. She picked up the belt from the counter and began to spank her. I knew I couldn't afford to look for too long, but lowering my head took a huge effort. The spanking, her bare bottom arched over, the wisp of hair peeking out between her thighs – it set me on fire. For months, almost every day, I fantasized, and masturbated about what I had seen and heard, every moment broken into exquisite detail.

It was the next spring before Joe and I crept out to the bathroom window again. We were tossing the football in his front yard, the door was open in the warm weather, and I heard Mrs. McFarland yell "I'm getting the belt." I shot a quick glance at Joe. Again, I followed him around the outside of the house until we reached the window. I motioned for him to straighten up and take a look, then became impatient when he kept looking. As soon as he lowered his head, mine was on the way up.

The slats of the blind seemed narrower, but I could see. Mrs. McFarland was standing and had Connie bent forward with her arm around her waist. Her shorts and panties were at her ankles, the belt hung from her mom's hand. I was again staring directly at the beautiful curves of her round, white bottom, and a wisp of hair peeking from between her thighs, as Mr. McFarland raised the belt and brought it down with a slap.

Mesmerized, my cock rock hard, the fog of arousal washed through me, and I was a split second slow as Ms. McFarland suddenly turned her head back toward the window. I dropped as fast as I could but I had seen her eyes.

"Damn."

"What happened," Joe whispered.

"I think she saw me. Your mom."

"God we better hope not." Joe started creeping quickly along the side of the house, staying low, and I followed. When we reached the front yard he grabbed the football and we started tossing it. We didn't say a word to each other.

Ten, maybe fifteen minutes went by and then I suddenly heard Mrs. McFarland's voice. "Get in here…both of you…now!" What I won't ever forget is what I faced as I turned toward the front door.

She was standing on the small front stoop, her long slender legs parted and bare half way up her thighs beneath her short, light blue robe, the belt hanging by her side, doubled in her hand.

She let us pass her through the door, then stepped in behind us and closed it. Her fierce expression forced our eyes to the floor. "Well, I hope you enjoyed watching me punish your sister, because you sure aren't going to enjoy the whipping I'm about to give you. You're not going to be able to sit for a week, and that's before your dad comes home and takes you to the garage with the strap. I've already called him. Get upstairs Joe, now."

Joe quickly climbed the stairs as she turned her attention to me. "Sit down in that chair and don't move Wally." I quickly did as she told me, but couldn't resist a peek as she neared the top of the stairs in her short robe.

I heard some serious yelling from Mrs. McFarland, then the slap of the belt. It sounded serious, and it went on for some time, with Joe occasionally crying in protest. I was scared…no doubt…at the thought of what might happen next. But I remember I was also rock hard.

Joe must have gone into the upstairs bathroom because he didn't come back down the stairs. "Wally, come up here."

When I entered the bedroom she was seated on the edge

of the bed, not more than six or seven feet from the door of the small room. Her legs were crossed and the belt was still in her hand, stretched across her lap. "Do you know that peeping in a window is a serious crime? Do you know that people go to jail for that?"

"Uh…I didn't know."

"Do your parents spank you, Wally?"

"Uh…sometimes."

"Do you want me to call your parents, or take you home, and tell them what you did?"

"No Mam. Please don't."

"Then we'll take care of your punishment right now and then we'll forget it. Is that what you want?"

"Yes, Mam."

"You know you deserve to be punished, don't you?"

"Yes, Mam."

"Pull your shorts down, Wally."

I didn't hesitate…and pulled my gym shorts down to my knees. "Pull then down to your ankles." I did as she said, then straightened up and put my hands across the front of my jockey shorts to hide the bulge. "Put your hands by your side." Again, I did as she said.

Mrs. McFarland uncrossed her legs and spread them to the width of her shoulders. Her robe hiked up, opened, and I was staring at the red thatch of hair. "Come over here," she said, in a clear, commanding voice.

I moved forward until I was right in front of her, my

eyes riveted between her legs. She reached out and slowly pulled my underpants down. I instinctively covered myself, then she quickly slapped my hand with the belt. "Put your hands by your side."

Again I did as I was told. My erection stood straight out. I was terribly embarrassed, but …definitely aroused. She stared at my cock for a few moments, then said, "Lay across my lap."

She parted her legs even more, and I was careful to lower myself so that I didn't touch her with my erection, positioning it between her thighs. I'll always remember the smell of alcohol on her breath, the touch of her hand as she gently placed it on my bottom, then the sting of the first blow. There were many more, and they came quickly. The spanking hurt, but there was another, dominant sensation – the hypnotic trance of spiked arousal. After a few minutes Mrs. McFarland stopped. I felt her legs move under me, then close tightly against my cock and balls. I'm sure I gasped. The belt started hitting my bottom again…and again…and then I exploded.

Cum shot everywhere, splattered on my arm, and for an instant I was mortified. But the waves and convulsions of ecstasy were so strong, and mixed with the blows that in my state now felt almost like caresses – I was paralyzed. I lay still across her lap, while she continued to spank me.

I don't know how long it lasted. I was completely spent, in a sort of dream, spread across her legs. At some point she told me I could get up, and as I stood I quickly came to my senses and yanked my underpants and shorts up. She got and left the room, never looking back as she said, "You can go now. Don't peek in my window again."

End of story. My first orgasm with a girl. Well, actually, a forty year-old-woman, lying across her lap while she spanked me. At that impressionable, sexually developmental age, I was already highly turned on by the erotic aspects of discipline. And now...

Hard to Believe

"You've got to be kidding."

"Pull your jeans and panties down and get across my lap. I'm going to give you a good spanking. It's much more effective than fighting and not speaking to each other for days"

"My God, Rob...you have got to be kidding me."

I remember the exact words...can see the scene unfold...as if it happened yesterday. But it's been three years, and I'm waiting for Rob to come home from work, and in the words he used this morning, "Take my belt off and tan your behind."

I still get angry that I'm subjected to being punished this way. But I've come to realize that the embarrassment and sting is mixed with a component of arousal. Is that because of the potent erotic brew, according to Rob, of the anxiety of knowing and waiting, the ritual of removing my skirt or pants, the preparation, being ordered into position, having my panties pulled down? Or is it thoughts of the incredible warmth, tenderness and sexual excitement and pleasure that he always gives me after my punishment is over. Doesn't matter. I'm at peace with it. And I have to admit that Rob was right from the beginning. The level and intensity of my sexual pleasure is greater with him than it has ever been at any other time in my life. I'm more in love him than I've ever been. But that flash of initial anger still flows through me when I'm told I'm going to be spanked.

I wonder if my punishment tonight will be the first episode for the blog. Another issue I fought against. And finally gave in. At least on a trial basis. After all, he's been right before. He promised I'll get to write as much of it as he does. From my perspective. Even if it's negative. Which presents me with a lot to mull over.

Of course we won't use our real names. He's going to be…hah…Victor. And we'll have disguises. We bought a dark wig and beard for him and a dark, short wig for me. There will be a single, small, unrecognizable corner of the house where we'll take the single photo that will go along with each journal entry. No more than one. I insisted. And absolutely no way to identify us or the house. I must admit - this elaborate production and writing all sounds like it could be fun.

But will I write what I really feel? That I hate it when I know I'm going to get a spanking. Or that I don't really hate it. That I often get wet when I think about it. But what part of it? Do I know what I really feel? Well, that's what I'll write…that I don't know. Or I don't think I know. I'll describe my feelings for each episode exactly as I remember them…as the episode plays out.

After dinner Rob disappeared for about twenty minutes and then reappeared in our office, where I was doing some work. He unbuckled his belt and slowly removed it. "Kate, follow me. It's time for me to discipline you."

I followed him downstairs, pretty sure now why we weren't going up to our bedroom or into the bathroom, the usual places where Rob takes me when I'm going to be punished. I followed him into the storage room. The chair against the wall and camera on the tripod confirmed my suspicions.

There was a box on the floor by the camera, and the wigs and his beard were inside. There was a new pair of panties – white cotton, legs cut high, but basically a "boy" cut, that I would never wear under normal circumstances. But then no one would assume I would either. He thinks of everything.

I had on tight jeans and a short sweatshirt, and he told me to take the jeans off, put the white panties on, then put the jeans back on. He told me to put on the wig, then grabbed his wig and beard and left the room. I was suddenly excited. As I pulled off my pants and thong and put the cotton panties on I felt moisture between my legs. There was a mirror on the wall opposite the chair and fitting the short, dark brown wig over my long blond hair was fun. I must say, I thought I looked pretty good as a brunette.

Rob came back into the room in full beard and toupee. He looked like a terrorist and I giggled. "I don't appreciate your humor when I have to discipline you. I don't think you'll find the spanking I'm about to give you funny."

He turned the camera on, then fired one test shot from the remote, igniting the flash. "Pull your jeans down."

It's ten in the morning, I've been sitting at the computer for an hour…and have just a couple of lines typed. On this, the day after the first episode that will appear on the blog, based on my punishment and our lovemaking last night - I need to get my entry finished before my noon appointment.

Last night was a real turn on…the sex was fantastic. I was dripping wet while Rob was spanking me, but it may have been the whole idea of the disguises, the blog, that others would know although we would remain anonymous. Maybe even I have some exhibitionism in me…if I can remain incognito. I want to write my true feelings, but I can't mention the blog because that would make it seem staged. No…I'm wrong. Of course I can.

Now I have a direction. I'm energized. My fingers begin to fly over the keys.

The idea of letting all the interested online world know that my husband spanks me like a naughty girl, the details of my punishments, and also our lovemaking, was not appealing to me when Victor first brought it up. I'm not sure how I got to this point…but Victor is very persuasive.

Yesterday was spent with the anxiety of knowing that Victor was going to discipline me when he got home from work. It sometimes happens when he first arrives, just after he's kissed me… signaled by the slow removal of his belt from his trousers, or sending me to get the hairbrush. It may happen after we have had dinner; a dinner during which I have a hard time relaxing, or enjoying the food and wine, knowing what I am in for.

There are few moments my impending punishment is not on my mind on the days I will be disciplined. I visualize what will happen…think about other times…again and again. A strange sort of tension stays with me all day. I'm still nervous on one level…but also feel an unmistakable, pleasurable stirring in my loins.

I had a dinner to squirm and attempt to act cheery and

nonchalant through. As soon as the dishes were cleared, I walked into the office. Victor followed in a few minutes and I looked up as he slowly unbuckled his belt and slid it out of the loops on his trousers, all the while staring sternly back at me.

"I'm going to discipline you now, Kate. Follow me."

Victor pulled the straight backed chair away from the wall, turned it to face me, and sat down. At least I was going to be across his lap. A slight bit of consolation for me, as I prefer the more intimate feel against his body as opposed to bending over or laying across the bed on my stomach – positions he often orders me into when he is going to spank me with his belt. When I'm across his lap I can feel his rock hard cock.

He told me to pull my pants down, and I quickly unbuttoned and unzipped them, squirmed and pushed until the skin-tight, faded jeans were below my knees. The lecture about my failure to keep to my prescribed workout schedule was familiar, as I stood before him with only my white cotton Jockey "boy" panties for cover. The fabric was molded to my body and I knew the mound of my unshaved pubic hair, that Victor insists I keep, was visible.

He motioned for me to lie across his lap. As soon as I was positioned, with my toes and fingers touching the floor, he slowly pulled my panties down below my knees. As always, he at first rested his hand gently on my behind and his fingers began slowly caressing...then tracing the crevasse between my cheeks...then slipping down and ever so lightly brushing across my tiny opening. That part I love. But then I felt the first slap of his belt on my bottom. That part – the actual spanking – I don't like, or at least I don't think I do. It stings...and I feel humiliated...embar-

rassed. But I also, inevitably, feel wetness between my legs...and know I'm turned on.

The spanking continued, and I began to squirm. Victor told me to remain still. After every ten or so slaps he stopped for a few moments and again gently caressed my stinging bottom. His fingers slipped between my cheeks and circled, probed and gently pushed against my anus. They slid down and across the lips of my pussy and inside the folds. Heaven had returned.

At this point there was no way to tell how much the spanking, which I mostly think I dislike, was responsible for my being so turned on. Love...hate...relationship? Who knows. The fact remains that I was incredibly aroused, and I knew that the lovemaking that would follow my punishment would be sublime and end in an enormous, shattering explosion of pleasure. Victor is a very proficient disciplinarian – but also an incredible lover.

My behind had a warm tingle all over it by the time the spanking ended. Victor's fingers were suddenly rubbing lotion into the reddened skin, expertly massaging my bottom, then following the familiar path down between my cheeks. Next the folds of my dripping pussy were gently stroked before his fingers slipped deeper inside. After untold minutes of this bliss, he eased me off his lap, onto my stomach on the floor, spread my legs, and his tongue began to slide between the cheeks of my behind. I was wild with lust as he nibbled and flicked his tongue across my anus. His fingers had found my clit, and his expert, velvet touch took me even higher.

Victor's patience is amazing. His fingers shifted to my bottom, his tongue to probing inside my pussy, another hand brushing across my nipples and breasts. It went on and on...and on. Waves of serene pleasure washed over me. At some point his tongue moved to my engorged clit...and flicked back and forth...and gently sucked. Did minutes go by...or hours...before I felt the long, thick, slightly bent shaft of his dick push up inside my dripping pussy from behind. A white hot, shuddering explosion happened all too quickly.

I'm not sure how many long minutes it took me to return to the world and think to ask him to turn the camera off.

And now, as I close, a thought flashes through my mind. When Victor talked me into accepting his form of discipline, I demanded that it work both ways. He didn't have much choice but to agree. It's been quite a while and the list of his missteps and neglect are considerable.

Judith's Story

On April 1, 1964, I was born to parents who were living the American Dream, overlaid on a template of beliefs and values held by dedicated Flower Children. I was named Judith, in honor of Judy Collins, one of the minstrels of the Age of Aquarius.

Mom was beautiful and Dad handsome, although her waist length, curly strawberry tresses and his golden, flowing locks and full beard hid much of their faces except when viewed head on. He was a successful record producer and she a sought after studio musician who could make a violin sing gloriously in any genre. They made excellent money, and we lived in an upscale neighborhood with large houses, acreage, and even a few barns and horses.

My childhood should have been perfect. In addition to a full range of creature comforts and the clear genetic link of looks and smarts, my parents provided a very relaxed child rearing environment. They loved me, but other than limited counseling emphasizing self-reliance and tolerance, there was little structure and practically no rules. They had many friends, partied with the best of them, and I, for the most part, was left to my own devices.

I was lonely, and with only one kid near my age on the street, I immersed myself in the world of books. Reading well by age six, and quickly tiring of children's material, I was devouring my parent's library by the age of ten. I remember precisely the first time I came across a reference to a spanking. Thumbing through the romance novels in the back corner of the drugstore while my mother shopped next door, I felt an immediate urge to touch myself. Spending time in that drugstore became a favorite pastime.

My fingers had already discovered pleasure between my legs, and I loved the smooth, gentle warmth that coursed through my body. Now, for the first time, there were images to think about…and the feeling was easier to start and extend.

Another favorite haunt was the local library, and my mother was only too glad to drop me off for hours of exploration. I learned to use the card catalogue and reference guides, and quickly found numerous facts and passages related to corporal punishment. Victorian authors were the best, with contemporary English writers a close second. But many American authors also mentioned my favorite subject, and of course I had the definitions from dictionaries and encyclopedias down pat. Newspapers and magazine articles were among my favorites, particularly those featuring celebrities remembering their teens. These were spankings that actually happened. And it was hard to find a romance novel in which the heroine didn't get threatened or spanked at least once.

I had plenty of friends at school, and there was no shortage of talk of the spankings and whippings that my classmates received or were threatened with. It was a badge of honor with many. I listened as if on a clandestine mission, asking questions until I thought it would arouse suspicion. I had real life images now, kids I knew. These images, along with what I read, provided fertile ground for explorations between my legs in my room. I didn't have much of an understanding of the sex act, or even the concept of sexual arousal, but I knew I could generate a very pleasant tingle whenever my mind turned to anything related to spanking, and that the feeling would intensify if I was able to slip my finger between my legs.

Living in a house void of rules or discipline, I was unsure if I wanted my parents to spank me. But I was sure I wanted someone to.

Elaine Solomon was the neighbor kid, and we started spending more time playing together after we ended up in the same sixth grade class. I was becoming quite devious, and it wasn't long after we started playing intense games of Crazy 8s that I suggested that the loser get a spanking from the winner. Elaine remained silent and her expression revealed little, but after my relentless goading, she agreed. I thought it would be a good time to ask if her parents spanked her. She said not very often and I decided to leave it at that...for then

I planned to set the rules and precedent by losing the first game, and as soon as it was over I said, "OK, you get to spank me." Elaine didn't look too excited, but I stood up, pulled my skirt up, and told her to turn around and sit on the end of the bed. As soon as she did I draped myself across her lap, with my bottom squarely over her legs. I waited. The first slap was light.

"If it's going to be a real spanking you have to pull my underpants down," I said. Without a word her fingers hooked on the waistband and she pulled them down to my knees.

I can still remember the exciting feeling of the air

rushing across the skin of my bottom, and then the spanking. I had to tell her she could spank me harder, and she did. It felt good, almost as good as I had hoped. When she lost and I returned the favor I was very methodical in pulling up her skirt and lowering her underpants, then marveled at the smoothness of her bottom and the beauty of the gentle curves.

We played cards with similar punishments a number of times over the next few months, Elaine quickly became an eager participant, and I even engineered a couple of games of doctor. But her mother burst into the room unannounced the day I brought the thermometer from home...just after Elaine had followed my instructions and pushed it into my bottom. Enraged, Mrs. Solomon stared me down as I scrambled to get my underpants and shorts back on. She called my mother and angrily stated what a horrible influence on her poor little Elaine I was, banned me from their house, and slammed the front door as soon as I was through it.

When I sheepishly walked into my house, my mother said calmly, in her soft, feathery voice, "that thermometer, as well as everything else in the medicine cabinet, is not for playing. Please don't take anything in the cabinet out of the house again."

The Stoop family moved into the house down the street when I was thirteen and in the eighth grade. I was soon spending many hours at their house. Maureen and her brother Martin were twins, one year ahead of me, in their second year of high school.

Maureen and I bonded and quickly became good friends. We spent hours in her room listening to records, talking about boys, or holed up in the cozy tree house nestled in the huge, split trunk of a giant willow in their backyard.

I had probably been hanging out with Maureen for a month when I rang the bell at her house after school one day – my usual routine. The door opened and Mrs. Stoop filled it. She was a tall, reasonably attractive woman, with a slightly stern appearance, as she usually had her black hair pulled back in a bun. "Hello Judy. I'm sorry, but you can't come in today. Maureen has neglected her chores, and then lied to me, and that kind of behavior isn't tolerated in this house. I'm going to punish her. If she acts like she's learned a lesson, perhaps you can come back tomorrow."

I was in a fog as I walked home, stumbling once over a tree root, my mind racing. *"I'm going to punish her". What did she mean? Being grounded? Surely not for only one afternoon. If longer, she wouldn't have said I could come over tomorrow if she "learned a lesson". What kind of punishments are there that can be handed out in one afternoon? Maybe extra chores.*

It was hard for me not to think of Maureen and her punishment while I was eating dinner and finishing my homework. I hesitated, then decided to call her. Mr. Stoop answered and told me Maureen couldn't come to the phone because "she's being punished." For a few moments I was sure she had only had privileges taken away from her. But then the images returned.

When I was in the safety of my room before crawling into bed, I let my mind fill with images of Mrs. Stoop giving Maureen a spanking. Then, even better, Mr. Stoop.

He was a bank president and handsome in a very preppy sort of way. Dark, thick hair, smooth, pale skin, horn-rimmed glasses. Maureen had the same pale complexion, a very pretty, dainty face ringed by wavy black hair, and a cute figure just short of plump. As I sat on the bed I suddenly got up, pulled off my pajama tops and bottoms, and stood in front of the full length mirror on the closet. My hands slid over my small but growing breasts, then around the soft curves of my bottom, through the emerging blond thatch of hair, and to that special spot between my legs. I had recently discovered the pleasures and beauty of many parts of my body, these sessions in front of the mirror were becoming a regular ritual, and the images I now had in my mind elevated the warmth that flowed through me to a dreamlike state.

Maureen was in her front yard playing with their dog after school the next day, and I made a beeline for her. "Hi, is it OK for me to come over?"

"Yeah."

"So what did you do yesterday to get in trouble?"

"I didn't clean my room, then told my mother that I had started cleaning it when I hadn't."

"I called last night and your dad wouldn't let me talk to you."

"Yeah, I know."

"So what did they do to you?"

"I got a spanking." I felt my face tighten and flush. I fought to show no change of expression.

"You get spanked?" I said, trying to act nonchalant.

"Oh yeah."

"Did your mom spank you?"

"Yesterday…yeah."

"Did it hurt?"

"Uh huh…but not too bad. Not as bad as when my dad does it?"

"How often does he spank you?

"Like…why are you so interested? Why so many questions?"

"My parents don't punish me…ever. For anything. I want to know what's it's like." I had rehearsed the line of questions and options until I had them down cold.

"Never! God are you lucky."

I hesitated, trying to gage Maureen's willingness to tell me more, then decided to continue. "So how often do they spank you?"

"I don't know. Like…whenever they get really upset with me."

"What do they do?"

"What do you mean?"

"Like…what do they actually do when they spank you? What do you have to do?"

"My Mom makes me go get a switch from the willow tree. Then she takes me up to my room and uses it on me."

"Do you have to take your pants down?"

"Oh yeah."

"Your panties too?"

"Oh yeah. She pulls them down."

"What position do you have to get in?"

"You really like knowing, don't you? Really...you've never had a spanking?"

"Never. So I want to know what it's like."

"She makes me lay across my bed on my tummy. Then she spanks my bottom with the switch. I've got to go now and do my homework. I don't want to get another one."

"Does your Dad spank you the same way?"

"He uses a belt."

"Does Martin get spanked?"

"Oh yeah...more than I do." Maureen quickly turned and walked toward the door, then looked back over her shoulder. "See ya tomorrow."

There was not a night over the next few weeks when I didn't finish the day in my room, naked in front of my mirror, or laying in bed, caressing and playing with myself while I visualized Maureen, or Martin, or me, getting spanked by her parents. I imagined the fear when her mother ordered her to get a switch, the anxiety as she was in the yard and came back into the house, having to go to her room and the moment she had to take off her jeans and her panties were pulled down. The fantasies were delicious.

I managed to get other details out of Maureen, and learned that she would often know all day, or for a few days, when her Dad was going to give her a spanking. He would take his belt off, take her up to her room, make her take off her skirt or pants, and then lay across his lap. He would pull her panties down. I imagined laying across his lap myself, with my bottom exposed, waiting for the spanking to start, then raising and shifting my hips and exposing that special place between my legs to Mr. Stoop.

At some point I started visualizing Martin getting spanked more than Maureen. He was the ninth grade stud, a great football player whom all the girls were in love with. Handsome, not that tall, but muscular across his slender body, he had the same black wavy hair as Maureen. By now I knew about the actual sex act, even oral sex, but it was little more than a concept. During the times that Martin would join us in the tree house after returning from practice, he would often brag about girls who would let him feel their breasts and who "want to get in my pants". Often I would catch him looking at my body. I was intrigued.

On a Saturday afternoon later in the Fall, Martin climbed into the tree house to join Maureen and I. There was room for all of us to sit, barely standing room, and our legs touched. Martin, as was his custom, soon started teasing Maureen, this time about her "bubble butt." She turned to me and said, "Martin, Judy is interested in our spankings since her parents never punish her. Why don't you tell her how sore your bottom is after Dad gave the big, tough football star a whipping last night."

Martin had a stunned, pained look on his face for a moment, then looked at me with a sly smile and said, "Yeah...wow...he really whipped my ass with that belt. There are probably still marks." Standing quickly, turning around, he said "Want to see?" as he quickly pulled his gym shorts and underwear down. Just a few inches from my face was his smooth, white, muscular bottom. There were a few faint pink lines, likely from his Dad's belt.

"Martin, what are you doing?" Maureen squealed.

"Want to see something else?" He turned around quickly and for the first time in my life I was staring at a very erect penis. Inches from my eyes. It was surrounded by a patch of black hair, tilted slightly upward, was thick, swollen, had a large red head...and was beautiful.

"Do you want to touch it?" Martin asked.

Without answering I wrapped my hand gently around the shaft and slid my fingers slowly across the head. If felt hard...and full...yet also soft. It felt wonderful...exciting.

"Martin...God...I'm going to tell Daddy and he'll whip you a lot harder than he did last night."

"Go ahead, and I'll tell him you touched it and he'll take the belt to your fat behind too."

Maureen suddenly bolted from the tree house. I hesitated for a moment, my hand still around Martin's penis. Then I quickly followed her down into the yard.

A couple of weeks later my mother called me to the phone one afternoon - it was Martin. "Hi, Judy, I have some information I think you'll be interested in. Maureen and I really pissed Mom off this morning, she called Dad, and he's going to spank us when he gets home. Maureen has a piano lesson at 6:00 tomorrow night, so why don't you come over about 5:00, we'll go to the tree house, and when she goes in for her lesson I'll tell you all the details. I know you're interested."

My devious, manipulative mind had me at the Stoop's

house and in Maureen's room at 4:30, my pre-planning complete. Luckily it was a nice day. "Let's go to the tree house…it's beautiful outside," I suggested.

Once settled inside the wooden structure that was about ten feet above the ground, we giggled through some small talk as I waited to see if Maureen would bring up last night. She never did, and time was running short. As always, I was careful to be casual. "Have you gotten in trouble lately? You haven't mentioned it."

"As a matter of fact…like…you must have ESP or something. My Dad gave both of us a really hard spanking last night."

"What did you do?"

"Mid-term report from a couple of days ago that we both didn't get signed…because we both made a C. When we showed it to Mom yesterday morning she got really mad, then a lot madder when she found out we were two days late asking her to sign it. She called Dad."

"OK, you know I want to know. Tell me what happened."

"God, Judy…I don't really like to remember it."

"Please," I said with a smile and pleading voice.

"Oh well…still seems weird that you're so interested. When Dad came in the door from work he was furious. He called us both down from our rooms, told us we knew exactly what was going to happen and why, threw his suit coat on the sofa and took off his belt. He grabbed me by the arm and pulled me into the downstairs bathroom. He was so pissed he didn't take the time to take us up to our rooms. He yanked my skirt up, then pulled my panties down to my ankles and made me bend over and put my hands on the toilet seat. He spanked me hard, for a long time, and when it was over I realized he didn't even completely shut the door. I know they heard everything and I'm sure Martin got at least a peek if he had a chance. He'll kid me about that for months."

"Then did he spank Martin?"

"Oh yeah…And really hard. He was yelling.

"Do you have any marks?"

"I don't know. I was kinda sore last night."

"Can I see?"

"Judy…you want to see my bottom? Now that's weird."

I looked straight into Maureen's eyes. "It's not only the marks. I love the way your bottom looks. It's so cute. I wish mine was as round as yours."

"Bubble-butt?" Come on. I wish mine was like yours. It's round but not nearly as big."

"Pretty please?"

"You really think it's cute?" Maureen stood up, turned around, and pulled her pink short shorts and white cotton panties down to her knees in one quick motion.

The sight of her bottom made me feel even warmer between my legs than I already felt. The crevice and pudgy cheeks made a perfect heart shape, and her skin was snow white and silky smooth. I couldn't resist reaching out and touching it with my fingers, then I suddenly remembered what I needed to say. "No marks. He must not have spanked you that hard."

"You wouldn't say that if he had spanked you."

"Your bottom is beautiful, really sexy. Boys must love it."

"You guys in there?" It was Martin. Maureen quickly pulled her shorts and panties back up and sat down, then tossed me a wry smile.

Martin climbed into the tree house, then eased himself down into a sitting position. "Man...my butt's sore. Did Maureen tell you what Dad did to us last night?"

I played along. "She mentioned it."

"Well, she may not be as sore as I am. Dad and Mom both always spank me harder. And then there's all that padding she has. Right bubble-butt?"

"I heard you yelling, big hero. Your behind was red as hell...I saw it when Dad came out of the door."

"At least I didn't cry like a baby and beg him to stop."

"Maureen...it's time for your lesson." Mrs. Smoot's voice sounded impatient. Maureen shot Martin a quick, slightly surprised glance, then me, then crawled down from the tree house. Martin stared at me without saying a word until he heard the door slam.

"So...what do you want to know?"

"Is that the hardest spanking you've ever had?"

"Close. Want to see if there are marks?"

"Yeah."

He stood, turned around, then slowly pulled his high school gym shorts and BVD style underpants all the way down to his ankles. There were a few lines that could have been from the belt, but again, they were faint. Martin's bottom was much slimmer and more muscular than Maureen's, and even more alluring. I raised my fingers and touched the silky skin, then traced down his crack. It wasn't long before he turned.

His magnificent penis was again only inches from my face. He didn't have to tell me what to do as I gently wrapped my fingers around the shaft. I noticed the very full sack hanging just below and brushed my other hand underneath it. Martin groaned. "Why don't you put it in your mouth?" he asked, "it will taste really good."

There wasn't much of a thought process. I just moved my hand and slowly let the length of his penis slip deep into my mouth. I began to slide my mouth up and back. I don't know whether I heard Martin's groan before I felt him quickly pull back and away, but something white and warm exploded across my face and blouse. He leaned back against the wall of the tree house and I watched as his penis convulsed and continued to squirt, then drip large white drops. His eyes were closed and he moaned softly. I put my finger to my cheek and gathered some of the white, sticky stuff, then put it in my mouth. It had a salty, thick taste. I knew what it was. I wasn't repulsed. OK...I liked it.

Neither of us said a word, but we knew we had to clean up quickly. I wiped my face with the sleeve of my blouse and Martin rubbed the spots into the wooden floor with his tennis shoes, which he still had on. His pants were still down and his penis smaller than before, but as I moved to him and wrapped my hand around it again I felt it start to swell. Suddenly I knew I had to get home as fast as I could.

A number of my fantasy sessions in front of my mirror, as well as daydreams, were now consumed with images of Martin's gorgeous penis sliding into my mouth, cradling it in my hands, and running my fingers across the cheeks of his bottom. Having it go into me between my legs seemed a bit problematic, as it seemed too large when it was hard. But I was intrigued.

Many of my visuals, however, were now fixated on Mr. Stoop giving me a spanking. I had all the details of exactly what happened when he spanked Maureen, and it was easy to substitute images of me, and my soft, white bottom. I felt a shudder when I pictured him telling me he was going to give me a spanking. The waiting would be tense, scary, but exciting. He would take me by the hand and lead me up to the bedroom. That moment when he would order me to pull up my dress and pull down my panties was delicious. And then when I pulled them down and bent over, exposing my behind and the new, silky hair between my legs... A strategy began to emerge in my devious, manipulative mind.

I conditioned myself not to be disappointed if it took two, three, maybe more weekends to find a day when everything was in place. It was the third Saturday when I knocked on Maureen's door, the flask in my backpack, along with my swim suit and towel for their pool. Mr. and Mrs. Stoop were in the living room, and I could hear Martin talking on the phone as I went up to Maureen's room

"Let's go to the tree house. I've got a surprise. I'm going to get Martin," I said as I walked out of Maureen's room and down the hall.

Martin was in his gym shorts on the phone, and I gave him a sly smile as I announced in almost a whisper, "Come on, we're going to the tree house. I've got something you'll like."

I had learned not only the pleasure but the power my blossoming body could give me, and I made sure I climbed up the six steps to the tree house just ahead of Martin. He had a clear view of my panties under my short summer jumper.

"Okay, what's this big surprise?" Martin said.

I reached into my pack, slipped the silver flask out, and held it out to Martin. "Have some of this...it's great."

His face lit up. "What's in there?"

"Jack Daniels. From my folks bar."

"No Martin, not here. If Mom and Dad find out..."

"Jesus. Come on, have some fun. Judy's cool. Why aren't you cool, Sis?" Martin unscrewed the top and took a swig, then passed it to me. I passed it back to him after I took a gulp, and after he turned up the flask again, he once again held it out for Maureen. She took a tentative sip.

After another round, I suddenly stood up, took a quick step toward the door and ladder, and said, "Gotta go to the bathroom...quick." I bounded down the stairs before anyone could say a word.

I walked through the back door to the house, into the bathroom off the kitchen, waited for a few minutes, then walked back out and into the living room.

"Hi, Mrs. Stoop," I said, standing just in front of her as she sat reading.

She looked up and her expression quickly changed. "Judy, what's that I smell?" Standing up, she moved very close to me. "Is that alcohol? Honey, come down here… right now!" Her voice was close to a scream

"What…what's wrong," I said, making sure my breath reached her.

Mr. Stoop suddenly walked into the room, clad in a pair of seersucker pants and golf shirt. "Judy's got alcohol on her breath. She's been in the tree house with Maureen and Martin."

"I can smell it. Follow me…both of you," he said in a steely voice, as he walked into the kitchen and out the back door. Mrs. Stoop pushed me forward with her hand on my back, and I felt a lump in my throat and tingle flash through my body as I followed him into the back yard.

"Martin, Maureen, get down here…right now," Mr. Stoop's voice boomed as he took long strides toward the tree house.

Maureen stepped down the ladder first, with Martin right behind her. Mr. Stoop moved to within inches of his daughter. "Breathe out, Maureen…now!" She began to cry. "Daddy…I'm sorry. Judy brought it…and Martin made me drink it."

Mr. Stoop stepped back a few feet, unbuckled the black leather belt he was wearing, pulled it out of the belt loops, and doubled it. "Get in the house…both of you. Right now!"

Maureen and Martin walked quickly ahead of Mr.

Stoop, and once again Mrs. Stoop nudged me in the back and we brought up the rear. I tried to remain calm, but felt my pulse racing. Once in the kitchen Mr. Stoop stopped and turned toward his children. "Get up to your rooms. And you better be ready for me to tan your behinds when I get up there. I want you lying across your beds with your shorts and underpants off."

There was no sound from either of them as they turned and walked toward the stairs. After a few moments Mr. Stoop turned to me. "Did you bring the alcohol?"

"Yes sir."

"Where did you get it?"

"From my parents bar."

"We're going to call your parents…and I hope they will punish you as thoroughly as I'm going to punish Martin and Maureen."

"They won't do anything to me."

"What?" What do you mean they won't do anything, " Mrs. Stoop said with a look of amazement on her angry, red face.

"They never punish me. They won't do anything."

Mr. Stoop spoke quickly. "You'd be a lot better off, Judith, if your parents gave you a thorough spanking when you misbehave. Martin and Maureen won't be able to sit down for a couple of days when I get through with them. We're going to call your parents and suggest they do the same to you."

"They won't punish me." There was silence for a moment. "But I think you're right, Mr. Stoop. I think I

need to be punished. I think it would do me a lot of good."
I paused. "I think you should give me a spanking."

There was a long silence, as Mr. Stoop first looked at
his wife, then leveled his stare at me. "Get out of here,
Judith, right now. And if it were up to me you wouldn't
come back."

Tears rolled down my cheeks and my mind raced as I
walked home. I was embarrassed...felt ridiculous...
angry...stupid...for trying such a devious and bold plan. I
pitied myself for being so *different*. There were now two
houses in the neighborhood...with my friends...where I
wouldn't be welcome.

That night, after I lay awake for hours agonizing over
my failures and seemingly overwhelming and enduring
problems, my hand slipped between my legs as my mind
suddenly shifted. I was now visualizing myself just inside
Maureen's bedroom door, staring as she still lay across the
bed, her panties around her ankles and her bottom a bright
pink from the spanking her Dad had given her. She
followed his orders, got up and quickly left...and I
followed his orders, stepped out of my shorts, and lay face
down across the bed. Mr. Stoop slowly pulled my panties
down to my ankles, his belt doubled in his other hand. I
spread my legs slightly, and imagined that the pause was
caused by his stare at my firm, round white bottom, and the
patch of golden hair visible between my legs. Then my
spanking began.

Two weeks before my fifteenth birthday my world
crashed. My parents were flying back from a recording
session on a private plane that went down in a
thunderstorm. The pilots, the rock group, and my parents

were all killed. There were no survivors.

The memories of those two weeks are mostly a blur. The sheer horror of the sudden tragedy...the funeral...deep depression. Maureen's parents were wonderful and had me stay with them from the first night. My uncle John was also around from the beginning, made all of the arrangements for the funeral, and comforted me and checked regularly to be sure I had everything I needed during this difficult time.

Uncle John was my Dad's only sibling, and our only relative that could be considered *close*. Both my Dad's parents had died relatively young, when he was in his early and late twenties, and my Mom's mother had died of cancer a couple of years ago, a few years after she divorced my grandfather, who had morphed into a sixty year-old Buddhist living on a sailboat in Europe.

Uncle John was the opposite of my Dad in many ways. A decorated fighter pilot during the Vietnam war, he now owned a successful company that leased private planes and helicopters. Somewhat shorter, more compact and muscular than my Dad, he acted very much the retired Major, with his blond hair worn in a short, military cut, and his square jaw and sparkling blue eyes highlighting a handsome face. Still exceedingly adept at giving orders as a civilian, Uncle John was one of those men who could get things done quickly and efficiently.

He had visited us a couple of times a year while I was growing up, and I had met his only child, Brett, when we were both younger. John and his first wife had divorced shortly after he returned from Vietnam, and he had remarried only a few years before my parent's death.

It was decided I would live with Uncle John, his wife Natalie and son in their house outside of Chicago. I didn't have much of a vote in the decision, but then with such a lack of living, functioning family and close relatives – what choice did I have? Their home was old, classic, large and beautiful, in a section called Oakbrook. My room was lovely, with a poster bed and matching, cherry antique furniture. The ceilings were high, bordered with exquisite molding, and I had a large bay window that looked out on a thick forest.

In his brisk, no-nonsense way, Uncle John was very attentive to me during the first few weeks. There was definitely a soft side to him, but it manifested itself differently than in most of the adult men I had been around. His wife Natalie was also friendly, although a bit reserved. She was an elegant, stunning, raven haired beauty with a perfectly honed, voluptuous body. Brett told me Uncle John was forty five and Natalie thirty four.

Brett and I hit if off famously from the day I moved in. He always seemed to have a smile on his face, which was as handsome as his Dad's. He had the same thick, muscular build, and was closing in on six feet when he turned sixteen the week after I arrived. Before the first week was over, I felt like I had the brother I had often longed for.

"Have they told you the rules yet? And the consequences if you mess up?" Brett's question came while we were sitting at the breakfast bar in the kitchen. It was summer, Brett had not yet left for baseball practice, and as Natalie was a partner is an art gallery, she was often away from home when we weren't.

"No. Why don't you tell me."

"Well…since you're a girl…and not my Dad's real kid…you might get lucky."

"I'm waiting. Tell me."

"It probably won't surprise you that Dad is a strict disciplinarian. When I mess up he whips my butt."

The lump was in my throat immediately. I tried to gather myself…act casual. "Really? How often?"

"Oh…I don't know…not that often. I try to avoid it. And then Natalie…well that's a different story. I mean… she's not my Mom and she's really hot."

"She spanks you too?"

"Yeah. But I'm sure it's because he made her. At least the first time. And here's the really crazy thing. I'm pretty sure I heard him give her a spanking. Like the Air Force I guess. Strict discipline and everybody treated the same."

My head was spinning…out of control. I waited for a moment. "Okay…slow down. What do you mean about the first time she spanked you?

"Well…like…I didn't do something important that Dad had told me to do for Natalie while he was out of town. He told me over the phone that he was going to whip me when he got home, and that she was also going to punish me. About an hour after he got off the phone with her, she walked into my room with a hairbrush and told me he had ordered her to spank me. I decided I'd have some fun because she looked nervous…and she's really hot. She sat down on the bed and told me to get across her lap. I walked over in front of her and pulled down my shorts and underpants....before she told me to. I had a big hard-on. She just stared...didn't say a word...until I finally got across her lap. The spanking didn't hardly hurt at all, but she made it last for a while."

"Has she spanked you again?" I asked, still trying to act cool and calm.

"Yeah. I think it's a little game now."

"What do you mean?"

"Like...the first time she used the hairbrush she had on a long skirt. The next time she just used her hand. And had on a short skirt. My cock rubbed against her legs. It was all I could do not to cum." Brett's open discussion of his "game" with Natalie didn't come as a surprise. Since that first day when we talked for hours, he had been very open about his obsession and experience with sex, and I had reciprocated with stories of the tree house, Martin's gorgeous penis, and my newly discovered fascination with intercourse. I had never mentioned spanking.

"So how does your Dad spank you?"

"He has a leather strap that he keeps in his drawer. I have to bend over the desk in his office. Man...it hurts."

"Do you have to take your pants off? Your underpants?"

"Yeah."

"I want to watch." The words came pouring out before I thought.

"What? You want to watch? Like...what is it...you want to see? I can just show you," Brett said, reaching for the zipper to his jeans. "You don't have to wait."

"Well...maybe another time. I'd like to see that. But I want to watch her spank you."

"Only if I can watch you. Of course we don't know if you're going to get a whipping yet."

"I guess that would be fair. I've gotta go do homework now." As soon as I was inside my room I shut the door and locked it, stripped, and stood in front of the full, floor length mirror on my closet door. My breasts were now lovely and full, though not large, without even a hint of sag. The tiny nipples stood straight out. I had a narrow waist and flat tummy, which accented my broad hips and firm, round, behind, covered with white, velvety skin. The triangular patch of blond hair was thick, and my legs were muscular and well tapered.

I lowered myself to the floor in front of the mirror and spread my legs so I could see the pink, wet lips of my pussy as I started caressing it. I quickly became lost in images generated from my talk with Brett. After a few minutes of gentle bliss, I turned and raised up on my hands and knees so I could look back at the smooth curves of my round, arched bottom. Reaching back with one hand I spread the cheeks of my behind apart until I could see the tiny, pink, hidden bud. My fingers again found my special spot.

It was only a couple of days later when I accepted Brett's offer to rub the soreness out of my stiff neck. His hand was inside my blouse and bra within minutes. Over the next week, when Natalie wasn't around, we touched each other more boldly during some intense petting sessions. And then one evening Uncle John and Natalie knocked on my bedroom door.

"We have some rules and regulations around here that you will have to follow. As with all of life, there will be consequences if you don't." Uncle John had a pleasant look on his face, but as usual, was intense. They both sat on my bed as I sat at the desk. He looked straight into my eyes as he spoke. "I don't know if you've heard the term "spare the rod and spoil the child" – but I'm a firm believer. If you misbehave you will be punished, and your punishment may well include a spanking."

I didn't move from my position at my desk. My heart raced. *Stay cool.* "Uh…Okay."

"We are very fair, and we will be loving and kind parents to you…as if you were our own. But part of that love includes discipline when you need it. We hope you understand."

"Uh…yes. Yes sir. I do."

They got up and left.

"I want to watch,' I said after Brett told me Natalie was on the phone with his Dad, discussing the incriminating note he brought home from school for cheating. It was about a week after Uncle John and Natalie's visit to my room. "Are you sure she's going to spank you?"

"No…but I'd sure bet on it. Dad won't be back until Friday and he'll be pretty mad about this. He probably won't let me get off for that long. And of course I think it's a game with her. A perfect excuse."

"I'm going to be in your closet," I said as I quickly turned to go up the stairs.

"OK…but if you get caught I'm definitely going to get my chance to watch…remember what Dad told you…he'll give you a whipping."

The closet was on the wall beside the bed, on the opposite side from the bedroom door...which would be perfect if Natalie sat on the bed as Brett said she did. I waited for what seemed like a long time, with the door pulled to but not latched, until I heard someone walk in.

I stayed as still as possible, than cracked the door until I had a clear view. Natalie was sitting on the end of the bed in shorts that left all of her beautiful thighs exposed, with her side to me, and Brett was standing in front of her.

"Take your pants off." He followed her instructions and stepped out of the warm ups. "And your underpants." Slowly, he lowered his white briefs and stepped out of them. His penis was standing almost straight out. It was beautiful...large...thick...and hung at a slight angle to his left. The head was swollen, red, and slightly turned up... pointed toward me. I had felt it through his pants but this was the first time I had seen it in all its considerable glory... and I had the sudden urge to touch myself. On this rare occasion my self restraint won out.

"Over my lap." Brett very methodically lowered himself onto her lap, with his cock pressed between her legs and his body. She used her hand, and the spanking was not harsh. It was long. There were sharp sounding slaps, but I could see his buttocks and they were only pink after many, many strokes. Occasionally she would rest her hand on his bottom between strokes, and was obviously in no hurry. Brett sometimes arched his bottom, and I could see his balls and cock lift off Natalie's legs. When the spanking was finally over and he stood, his cock as hard and swollen as it was when he lowered his underpants, he turned slightly to face the closet, then stood still before reaching for his clothes.

Our petting session reached new frontiers the next day, as he pulled my panties down and licked between my legs. His tongue slid up and down the lips of my pussy, flicked in and out. A first for me. I tingled all over. It felt wonderful. Not wanting to seem ungrateful, I pulled his dick out above the waistband of his undershorts and licked it with all the skill I could muster. My first full taste of cum was an enjoyable one, as he exploded as soon as I pulled his underpants down and wrapped my hand around his balls.

It was the end of the week, Uncle John had just returned home in the evening, and he immediately went into his office and came out with a wide leather strap in his hand. I watched as he marched Brett back into his office, then listened as well as I could from the living room. There were slaps and muted cries. It indeed sounded like he got his "butt whipped." I now knew what would work and wasn't going to deviate and take a chance on failure.

It was easy to generate the catalyst. I missed a day of class, got on a bus and went to the mall - automatic note home and two day suspension. I asked Natalie to sign it so Uncle John wouldn't find out, knowing the dynamics of the relationship would work in my favor, but I didn't show it to her until just before he got home from work. I couldn't decide if I wanted her to spank me. I knew I wanted him to. Brett seemed fired up to watch, but also really scared because the closet in the office was in full view of the desk.

Uncle John didn't say anything through dinner, but as we were finishing dessert he looked directly at me with his steely blue eyes. "Judy, skipping school is a very serious offense around this house. I can't imagine what you were thinking. Please come to my office as soon as you are finished eating. We're going to have a little talk and I'm going to discipline you. And don't make me wait."

Brett and Natalie both looked at me. I felt like I was about to start shaking...my mouth was suddenly, incredibly, dry. "Brett, I want you in your room studying...right now. Your grades can still get much better."

I stood up, walked down the hall and into his office. Standing in the middle of the room, alone, not sure what to do next, I took stock of my feelings. It was about to happen...finally. I was going to get a spanking. But I was nervous. Excited...aroused....absolutely.   But nervous. Maybe even scared.

Uncle John stepped into the office and shut the door behind him. "Why did you skip school, Judy?"

"Uh...I don't know."

"Of course you know. And you had better tell me right now. This is out of character for you. You're an excellent student and haven't misbehaved since you've lived with us."

"I just didn't want to go. It's boring sometimes. I wanted to go shopping. I know it was wrong."

"Yes, it was. And you're not going to do it again, are you?"

"No. No sir."

He walked behind his desk, opened a drawer, and pulled out the leather strap. Looking me straight in the eye, he said, "I'm going to give you a spanking, Judy. You do remember our conversation about discipline, don't you?"

"Yes sir."

"So you expected me to punish you, right?"

"Uh…I guess. Yes sir."

Uncle John stepped from behind the desk, the strap in his hand, and moved the straight back chair to the side of the desk away from the desk…then turned it to face me. He sat down. "Lay across my lap."

I did as he told me. Once I was settled, my black and white saddle oxfords were touching the floor and my hands grasped the legs of the chair. I had on the just-above-the-knee plaid skirt and blue oxford shirt that was the uniform of the private school I now attended, and the skirt was riding halfway up my thighs. Uncle John began to lecture me on my misbehavior and how it wouldn't be tolerated, asked me again if I understood, then slowly raised my skirt above my waist. I wore a pair of high cut, white cotton panties, and the air felt cool on my thighs and the bottom of the cheeks of my behind that were exposed. He stopped talking for a few moments…it was very still and quiet… and then I felt his fingers slip under the waistband of my panties. The cool air hit my bottom as he pulled my panties down to my knees. I ignored caution and shifted on his lap, arched and spread my legs a bit, and the coolness slid between my thighs and the cheeks of my bottom. Again there was silence…no movement. Uncle John had an eye full of my behind and the blond hair and pink lips that were surely peeking out between my slightly parted thighs.

I waited…still nothing. Then he spoke, not quite as

loud and firm as before. "I don't want to spank you, Judy. But I will whenever I think you deserve it." The first blow was surprisingly light...but they quickly increased in force. After four or five strokes, the belt began to sting. He would hesitate after every four or five strokes ...and his hand occasionally rested gently on my bottom. The pain increased with the number and intensity of the strokes, but it was never severe and was overcome by the warmth and arousal coursing through my body. As my spanking continued, I was pretty sure the moderate pain contributed to the excitement. In any case...I was really turned on. As turned on as I had imagined. Maybe more so.

I knew I was wet, and I instinctively pulled my thighs together so Uncle John wouldn't see. His hand was still resting on my bottom between strokes, and he had not said anything for some time. He continued to spank me. I settled into a dreamy state of arousal; almost as if I were being given a sensual massage rather than an old fashioned spanking with a strap.

"You may get up now, Judy. I hope I don't have to do this again anytime soon. But I will." I didn't want to get up...didn't want it to be over. But I knew I needed to do as he told me. I did not want to give him any indication that the spanking had been anything other than punishment to me. He put the strap back in the drawer and walked from the room as I was still arranging my skirt.

As soon as I could get to the privacy of my room I stripped, turned and stared into the mirror at the lovely, pale shade of pink covering my behind, then lay on the floor and slipped my fingers between my legs. Thoughts of the spanking flooded my mind, and the familiar, luxurious, warm tingling consumed me within moments. I was dripping wet. The familiar sensations suddenly rocketed to an intensity I'd never felt. My whole body convulsed…and I shut my eyes and contorted my face to handle the surge of spasmodic pleasure coursing through my every fiber. When the rush subsided, I was left panting, wasted. I knew without any doubt that I had just experienced my first orgasm.

It was a couple of days later before Natalie was out of the house and Brett opened the door to my room and walked in. "You owe me, sis. Big time."

"What do you mean?"

"There was no way I could watch Dad give you the whipping the other night after he sent me to my room, and we had a deal. You watched me."

"Not my fault."

"You still owe me."

"What if I tell you about it."

"Please do. But you still owe me."

"It hurt…but not too much. He lectured me first, then got his strap and made me lay across his lap."

"You didn't have to bend over. Hm…sounds like Natalie. Do you think it turned him on?"

"I don't know. He did keep laying his hand on my bottom. Anyway…he pulled my skirt up and then pulled my panties down.." Brett was sitting next to me on the bed, and his hand was suddenly sliding up my thigh and under my skirt. His fingers went inside the elastic leg of my panties and touched me. I lay back on the bed.

He pushed my skirt up and pulled my panties off, then slid his tongue along the lips of my sex. Lifting his head, he moved to the door and locked it, then returned to the bed. I watched as he pulled off his shorts and underpants and the magnificence of his swollen, thick cock bobbed free in front of me. His tongue slid along my pussy for only a few moments before I felt his cock against my lips. Brett had tried before and I had refused...but I wasn't going to refuse this time.

There was a sudden, sharp pain, but it subsided into the beautiful sensation of being filled with Brett's gorgeous cock as he pushed slowly up into me. At first his thrusts were forceful but slow, then they increased in intensity and speed. The feeling was delicious and I began to move my hips in concert with his. This time I was pretty sure what was coming a few moments before my body clenched in a shattering climax. A few more thrusts as I was moaning and Brett's body also spasmed, then went rigid, before he collapsed onto my chest.

I was not a mischievous teenager by nature, but rather an excellent student and gentle soul. I had to be careful not to play my "bad girl" role too often, and cause suspicion, even though getting Uncle John to spank me became somewhat of an obsession.

The ritual was exactly the same the second time I was punished, about a month after the first time. The third time, there was a slight variation. I was sent into his office...he lectured me...and again took the strap from the drawer. Since I had on jeans he ordered me to take them off...then told me to bend forward across his desk. Following orders, my tummy and chest ended up flat against the desk and my hands grasped the edge. Uncle John then pulled my panties down to my ankles and gave me a firm strapping. The change in position was OK with me, and I had my usual explosive orgasm later in my room, but I preferred the intimacy of being across his lap. The next time he spanked me he went back to turning me over his lap and for the first time used his hand instead of the belt. He was in no hurry and I was in bliss, for quite a while. In between the stinging slaps, his hand lingered longer than before on my bottom.

The intensity of my arousal and orgasms, after a spanking or while reliving the punishment, was the best. But I was also capable of losing myself in the pleasures of sex without the stimulation of discipline. Brett and I usually found at least one or two afternoons a week when Natalie and Uncle John were out and we could play, and for months we conducted what was essentially a lab class for sexual variations. It may have started as 101, the introductory course, but it progressed to the 401 advanced class. We must have been light years ahead of other teens our age. And many adults. Intercourse was a favorite. But we were both adventurous, and in addition to enjoying giving and receiving oral sex, we discovered the pleasures associated with anal play. After using Vaseline pilfered from the master bathroom, Brett bought a tube of KY Jelly. I loved the feeling of the cool liquid being massaged around and into my bottom, then the sensation when his finger slid inside me. Giving Brett equal time and treatment with my fingers and tongue also gave me great pleasure. His body rippled with smooth muscles, his ass was tight, jutting and beautiful, and his cock a gorgeous sight when it was erect and throbbing. I never seemed to tire of playing with him...or being played with.

A number of months after my first spanking, Brett and I overheard a conversation that lent credence to his belief that his Dad might also punish his Stepmother. I was in my room one evening when Brett opened the door. "Follow me. And be quiet when we get in my room."

There was an elaborate intercom system in the house and Brett had it open to the recreation room in the basement. Uncle John and Natalie were talking and laughing with another couple, and if you listened carefully you could hear their voices above the music. We had to sift through the sounds of glasses, ice and the click of pool balls striking each other, but what we heard was definitely interesting.

"Chris, she's giving you a damned hard time. Again. She's not letting up. I can't believe you take that. Natalie knows if she talks to me like that I'll pull her panties down and spank her behind."

"Really." The voice was female. "Natalie?"

"Uh...come on, Darling...stop kidding." It was Natalie.

"You and I know I'm not kidding, Dear."

"Sounds pretty hot to me." The other female voice was pitched higher than Natalie's, and there was a slight accent. "I'd love it if Chris would spank me when I'm bad. But he won't even go down on me...that's too kinky for him. Maybe John could spank me. I am being bad. Natalie... would that be okay?"

"No...definitely not. Not a chance," Natalie replied quickly.

"Oh well, you never know till you try. Damn. More

frustration."

There were a few moments of silence. Then a male voice other than Uncle John's said, "It's your shot, Catherine…go ahead." The click of pool balls. Then more silence.

A few months after I turned sixteen Brett made the announcement that he had a girlfriend. It wasn't a surprise, as he had been hanging out with Megan, dreamy eyed, for a couple of weeks. A great catch for him. She was a cheerleader and gymnast, with a gorgeous face framed by long, thick dark hair, and a curvy but tightly muscled body. Neither one of us said anything about ending our regular sexual sessions…but they suddenly stopped.

A couple of months later I was standing at the sink in the kitchen and Brett was sitting at the breakfast room table, on a day Natalie was away. Suddenly, the words came tumbling out. "So…is the sex with Megan as good as it was with us?"

"No. No way." His words came quickly. There was silence for a few moments and then I was aware of the chair sliding back and Brett walking up in back of me. Pressing his crotch against my bottom, he slid his hand under my skirt.

My own lust and reading told me at an early age that I was highly sexual…and likely kinkier than most. But I knew right from wrong. "No, Brett. You can't treat her that way." I pushed back and went upstairs to my room. The two of us had conversations about sex on a number of other occasions, and he often got aroused. But he continued to go with Megan until he left for college, and we only talked.

One of the hardest spankings I received while living at Uncle John's was the only spanking that Natalie gave me. After six months in their house I was pretty sure she was leery and a bit jealous of the long looks and attention that Uncle John gave me. I could only imagine her anxiety, or anger, when he took me into his office to discipline me and the accepted ritual she surely was aware of – her husband pulling my panties down and giving me a lengthy spanking.

It was late one afternoon, Uncle John was out of town, and Brett and I were talking in the kitchen. My offense was minor…a load of clothes she had asked me to wash that I forgot. She said I had been slacking off on my household duties of late, which was not true. I knew she had another agenda. She made the announcement in front of Brett…thinking, I'm sure, that it would embarrass me.

"Judy, I'm going to punish you. Go up to my bedroom and bring me the hairbrush that's on the dresser." I did as she told me and when I returned with the wooden brush she took it from me and again spoke with Brett standing only a few feet away. "Go into the bathroom and pull your jeans down. I think a good spanking is exactly what you need."

I had just pulled my jeans off and laid them across the sink when Natalie walked in. She had the brush in her hand, walked past me, and pulled out the small chair from under the end of the vanity. She walked back to the door and before pushing it only partially closed said in a voice loud enough for Brett to hear, "Pull your panties down, Judith." She sat down in the chair and motioned for me to lay across her lap. With my panties and jeans now around my knees I shuffled forward and draped myself across her thighs…careful to press my thighs together. If I became wet I didn't want her to know. She was wearing slacks, not shorts or a short skirt.

The brush had a sharper sting than Uncle John's strap, and she spanked me for a long time. I felt the familiar warmth of arousal run through my body, and it spiked when I thought that Brett might be watching through the partially open door, or at least listening. But I was not as turned on as when Uncle John disciplined me. In a way I was glad when she quit. The force of the hairbrush landing on my bare behind told me she enjoyed it, and the sting began to outweigh the arousal. When Natalie finished she had me stand and she got up and walked through the door. After getting dressed I walked into the kitchen for some water, and Brett was waiting. He had watched, and his detailed description of my bottom squirming and turning a bright pink as Natalie paddled me made me wet. I went to my room quickly to avoid the temptation.

A couple of months after Brett's announcement of his love for Megan, I realized I may have received a double whammy. Playing my role as a misbehaving niece was no longer causing Uncle John to take me to his office for a spanking...even when I pulled out all the stops and again skipped school. I was only grounded...repeatedly.

There had been a hint of the change. The last time Uncle John spanked me, he seemed particularly upset. It was only the second time he told me to bend across his desk instead of laying across his lap. He raised my skirt, then pulled my panties down to my ankles and told me to step out of them. In this position I was able to spread my legs enough to give him a very clear view of my wet pussy, which I no longer tried to hide...and after ten or twelve fairly hard slaps of the strap across my bottom I felt his hand begin to gently massage my stinging cheeks. His fingers suddenly slipped along and into the crevasse, then slid lower, between my parted legs, and finally brushed lightly across the soaked lips of my pussy. Just as suddenly I was told, "Get dressed and go to your room. You're grounded for a week." He quickly walked from the room, leaving me still bent forward across the desk.

I also found love in the last year of high school. Bill was captain of the football team, tall, dark, and handsome. A hunk. Also very smart. He stole my heart, and within a month of beginning to "go together," we were having sex. It was good, but he was not the adventurer that Brett had been. A straight, chivalrous sort...he treated me exceedingly well. But he was deeply opposed to doing anything "weird." On the couple of occasions I misbehaved on purpose and playfully suggested that he might need to spank me – well, it was obvious he just didn't get it. Toward the end of my senior year the steady diet of vanilla sex with Bill was getting old. The decision to break up the summer before we went off to different colleges was a relief. I was ready for lots of big changes.

I earned a full academic scholarship to a prestigious, small liberal arts college in the Midwest. Majoring in English and French, with a minor in Spanish, would allow me to pursue my dream of teaching abroad or working in the diplomatic corps.

I worked hard my first couple of years, didn't find anyone I wanted to date more than a couple of times, and earned straight As in all my courses. My sex life was primarily limited to masturbation sessions, fueled by memories of being punished by Uncle John, afternoons of sexual experimentation with Brett, elaborate fantasies focused on being disciplined, then pleasured, by various authority figures, and the references to spankings that I still found with ease in various genres of literature. I did have the occasional one night college fling, but knew what I really needed.

I had mastered the role and description to any promising partner...of the spoiled, mischievous, impossible-to-control coed, who "probably needs a good spanking." Usually rewarded with "the stare," I faced reality. One of the few guys who did take me up on my request, and even seemed to enjoy it, was a bit heavy handed. It was obvious he didn't really understand the dynamic or rituals I was looking for, and I sensed he had a significant dark side. Once was enough.

The first semester of my senior year I took a contemporary literature class under Professor Anthony Montgomery. A classic Brit, he had been teaching in this country since receiving his doctorate from Princeton, and was in his late thirties. A handsome, chiseled, but ruddy face was partially hidden by a full beard, which flowed from a head of thick, curly brown hair. A tweed jacket, bow tie and pipe jutting from his breast pocket completed the look. He was extremely bright, quick and witty, challenged his students, and his accented voice began to randomly pop into my mind.

A couple of months into his course, he assigned a collection of short stories that had been awarded the distinction of "Best American Short Stories", published in an anthology under that name by leading educational publisher Houghton Mifflin. John Updike, Susan Sontag, and Joyce Carol Oates were but a few of the Pulitzer prize winners and world renowned authors whose works were included.

Professor Montgomery assigned two of the short stories each night, and we were to come to class the next day prepared to discuss both. The third assignment included *Exchange Value* by Charles Johnson, and *A Working Day* by Robert Coover. I settled in to my couch and flew through the first story, an interesting take on self entrapment in a closed, urban environment. Irony was my thing and Johnson wrote world class examples.

After making a cup of espresso, I launched into *A Working Day*. I sat up after the first few pages. I had a sense...but no...couldn't be. Then on page eight - I read it twice. A conversation in which an elderly gentleman questions if he is treating his young maid fairly...as he unbuckles his belt. Followed by a beautifully crafted description of his negligent employee shuffling steadily and contritely across the room to the bed, where she lifts her skirt, pulls her panties down, and bends over in preparation for a spanking.

Amazing. Damn. More than amazing. Robert Coover, renowned man of letters and author of novels, plays, film scripts, essays and short stories – he's like me. He gets it. It turns him on. Would have to...or he couldn't write it this way. And his damned short story about my fetish has been judged one of the best American short stories of the entire decade. And a huge and prominent publishing house published it.

I read every word...but searched with laser focus for the phrasing, descriptions, and vocabulary that told the tale I was looking for. As the story progressed, I was rewarded again and again.

The great writer drew vivid visions of the maid's

bottom being bared and then dancing to the varying tempos of her employer's discipline. And the positions, all highly traditional, that he ordered her to assume for her punishments. And his choice of his hand, a switch, hairbrush or strap. Perhaps my favorite images from his elegant narrative were of the gradually reddening hue of the maid's lovely buttocks as he applied what he accepted as prescribed punishments.

Falling asleep was difficult for me that night.

After forty five minutes spent discussing *Exchange Value*, Montgomery asked the class for comments on *A Working Day*.

"A weird old man who likes to spank his maid." Randy, a lacrosse star, chuckled as he spoke.

"Very good, Mr. Hall. But your analysis is a bit shallow, wouldn't you say? Anyone else?"

Victoria was the class know-it-all, very smart, and she could always be counted on to speak up. "He was so manipulative...and cruel. Playing on the feeble mind of someone desperate enough for salvation and godliness that she would endure the punishments."

I raised my hand, was acknowledged, and said, "The only way it makes sense is if she got something else out of it. Coover went to great lengths to give us only one hint of that – how often she screwed up."

Professor Montgomery stared at me for a few moments. "And what would that something else be?"

"Some level of physical or emotional stimulation or reward...beyond the religious implications. The author must have more than a passing knowledge of the subject."

Still staring at me, his voice was soft. "There are many references to the erotic aspects of corporal punishment throughout literature. Often reflective of the times. Many "Gentlemen" during the Victorian era were familiar with the rituals and pleasures associated with physically chastising their maids and servants. Ladies of the House also enthusiastically applied a birch switch or strap. Headmasters, until relatively recently, particularly in my native land, enthusiastically handed out punishment to the backsides of lads and lasses. Nuns and Priests have for centuries paddled their charges and students. Legions of husbands have disciplined their wives in this way. As the buttocks and loins are traditionally bared for corporal punishment, it is easy to see why there can often be a strong erotic component."

"Yes, it's obvious Coover is familiar with the subject. As are other well respected authors. And for those of you who aren't that well read...yet...maybe you've plowed through a romance novel. There's rarely a heroine in one of these works...I use the term generously...who isn't turned over someone's knee at least once in order to straighten her out."

"Very well...that's all for today. Be prepared again tomorrow. I thrive on educated participation."

A week went by before I allowed myself to knock on Professor Montgomery's office door one afternoon. I had been late in handing in an assignment a couple of days earlier, and missed class on that very morning. The deep, soft "Come in" caused a slight shiver to run through me. I pushed the door open and was in front of a cluttered desk in a room filled with overloaded bookshelves and books on every available surface.

"Miss Jensen. What can I do for you?" His eyebrows lifted slightly above the sparkling blue eyes, creating a quizzical smile.

"I've decided I want to apply to graduate school here, get a masters and likely a doctorate in English, and I would like for you to write a letter of recommendation and be my graduate advisor."

He stared at me for a moment. "And why have you come to this decision?"

"Your class has had a lot to do with it. I mean...I've thought about it for a while, but I've enjoyed this class so much. The literature, analysis and writing convinced me."

"Miss Jensen, I find it strange that you've picked a day you missed my class...and only a few days after you missed an assignment deadline, to ask me if I will be your major professor."

My mouth was dry. I waited...took my time...looked down at the floor. "I'm not the most disciplined person...and I know I need to improve. But I will. I promise. I'm hoping you can help me with my self-discipline as well as the literature, writing, and my development as a grad student."

"And why do you think I could help you with self-discipline?"

"Uh...I'm not sure. I just have a feeling you can."

"I'm an Englishman Miss Jensen. My ideas on the discipline sometimes necessary to attain an adequate level of self-discipline...are a bit traditional. Old fashioned if you will. Do you follow me?" His eyebrows again lifted as he stared at me intently.

"Yes...uh...yes, sir. I think I do," I said, as I continued to bet that I did.

"Very well...I'll give it some thought. Now excuse me, I must finish grading these essays," he said as his eyes turned quickly down to his desk.

Two of Montgomery's classes and a very long week passed before he tapped me on the shoulder and asked me to come by his office after class.

The door was slightly open, I knocked and walked in. "Close the door behind you, Miss Jensen." He did not ask me to sit down. "I've decided to accept your offer to write a letter of recommendation and be your graduate advisor...should you be admitted. But I'm not completely comfortable with your request that I help instill the discipline necessary for you to accomplish your academic goals." Montgomery stared at me for what seemed like a long time. "You may sit down Miss Jensen."

Stroking his beard while his eyes bore into mine, he seemed to hesitate before speaking. "I told you my ideas on discipline are traditional and old fashioned. Do you know what kind of discipline I favor?

"Uh...I think so."

"Tell me, Miss Jensen...what kind of discipline?"

"Well...uh...the kind that Coover wrote about in *A Working Day*."

"But the old man was sometimes quite harsh, Miss Jensen. You wouldn't expect that from me, would you?"

"Uh...no sir. I would hope not."

"I'm going to give you one more chance to rethink your

position. Take a day or two at least. And unfortunately, due to the extremely litigious nature of our culture and this country, should you still decide to move forward, you will need to sign this document..." He reached for a sheet of paper on his desk, handed it to me as his eyes were locked on mine, then stood up, and said "You'll have to excuse me now, I'm on my way home."

After Montgomery walked past me and into the hall, I picked up the single sheet of paper and followed. He shut and locked the door and I watched him walk toward the end of the hall to the right, I turned left, then right around the next corner, stopped quickly, and began to read.

AGREEMENT

I, _____**(Judith Jensen), have requested that Dr. Anthony Montgomery assist me in developing the self-discipline necessary to complete a rigorous graduate program in English. I have requested that Anthony Montgomery discipline me as he deems necessary, and that this discipline be corporal in nature on the occasions that he determines that I will benefit from such discipline.**

_____   _____
Judith Jensen   **Dr. Anthony Montgomery**

_____   _____
Date   **Date**

My hands were shaking as I quickly placed the document into my book bag. Walking back to the dorm I was so deep in thought and a slide show of images that I ran head on into another student and knocked his soft drink out of his hand.

After signing the document and sliding it under Montgomery's door the next morning, I attended the next two classes, then missed the third, a day that a written review was due. I brought the review to the next class, and when I handed it to Professor Montgomery he never looked up from the papers on his classroom desk and said, "Please see me in my office this afternoon Miss Jensen."

"Come in, Miss Jensen" His voice was steady, matter-of-fact. He didn't look up from his desk while handing me a single sheet of paper, then his eyes met mine.

"Please come to that address at 8:30 this evening. I think it is time to address your self-discipline issue." His eyes went back to his desk.

"Yes sir." He said nothing else. I turned and left the room

The rest of the afternoon and early evening went by very slowly. Images and scenarios flashed through my mind with lightning speed. Would he give me a spanking? Surely he would. How severe would it be? Was he an actor in my little play, or did he truly believe that corporal punishment was the most effective way to straighten up a lazy, irresponsible student. I was anxious, nervous, excited, aroused. All the feelings that always assaulted me before I knew, or even thought, I might be disciplined.

The house was a quaint bungalow in an old, in-town

neighborhood close to the college; the perfect home for a professor. I rang the bell, and after a short wait the door opened and Professor Montgomery appeared. He was dressed in a blue, button down collar cotton shirt, tan slacks and loafers. "Come in, Miss Jensen." He led me into a cozy living room and motioned for me to sit down in a leather arm chair. He took a seat on the sofa, across from me.

"You realize your absence from my class and neglect of the date your assignment was due are not the kinds of behavior that should induce me to write a convincing letter of recommendation for your admission to our graduate program."

"Uh...yes sir. I understand that."

"Miss Jensen, I was quite a problem as a young boy. Total lack of self-discipline myself. And very adventurous and contemptuous of authority. My parents, bless their hearts, were both in the art world, very bright, talented, but gentle people. They tried everything, and ended up shipping me off to a boarding school in Scotland for, shall we say - troubled youth. Best thing that ever happened to me. But it was a very tough place that highly valued strict discipline. There were both boys and girls, all teens, and when we misbehaved in any significant manner, we were all treated the same and sent to the headmaster. Unless there were extenuating circumstances, that usually meant we had to bare our bottoms and bend over his desk for a strapping. It was very effective. Particularly for the girls. It was a private school and their methods could not be questioned. We'll now see how you respond, although I'll be a bit more lenient than my old headmaster, at least in the beginning."

Standing up, he moved to the straight-backed, upholstered chair along the wall, then pulled it out into the center of the room and sat down. "Please lay across my lap, Miss Jensen."

His words sent a shudder through my entire body. My stomach tightened, I found no response, but stood up and slowly draped myself across his lap, my feet touching the floor on one side and my hands on the other. I had on a light blue cotton dress with a belt cinched tight around my narrow waist, and sandals with medium heels. After a few moments in this position my dress was pulled up tight against the belt and laid across my back, and then I felt his fingers slide under the waistband of my tight, white nylon panties, and slowly pull them down to just below my knees. I was sure goose bumps appeared on my bottom as the cool air caressed it. He said nothing for a few long moments. I shifted my hips just a bit and my thighs parted slightly. "I'm going to give you a thorough spanking, Miss Jensen. I hope this will be the first step in helping you change your ways."

The first blows seemed light, but they quickly increased in intensity. He alternated between my bottom cheeks and occasionally his hand landed across both of them. Even when the spanking was the most intense, with the blows coming rather quickly, I never felt pain that was not overshadowed by the delicious warmth and arousal coursing from my loins and throughout my body. It went on for a long time...or so it seemed. I shifted my hips occasionally, spreading my thighs a bit more, abandoning any serious effort to keep the wetness between my legs from him.

"Very well, Miss Jensen, you may stand up and

rearrange your clothes."

I slowly got up, pulled my panties up and my dress down. Montgomery stood up, moved toward the door, and turned back to look directly into my eyes. "I expect your behavior and self-discipline to improve, Miss Jensen. Good evening."

Confused, disappointed, hopeful, incredibly turned on – these feelings all washed through me as I climbed into my car and started back to the dorm. I couldn't ever remember wanting anyone to touch me as much as I had wanted Montgomery to…to caress me…make love to me. It didn't take long, remembering the details of the spanking, to explode in a shattering climax when I was alone in my bed.

Only a week went by before I was on my way to Professor Montgomery's house again. Missing class when an assignment was due was the key, but I did decide I would vary the crime in the future. I rang the bell, waited, then the door opened and he gave me a stern look.

"Come in, Miss Jensen. Sit down, please," he said as he motioned me to the couch. There was a hard tone to his voice. "The spanking I gave you last week obviously didn't accomplish what I had hoped it would. I won't be as lenient again." He was still standing, and started to unbuckle the wide, brown leather belt he was wearing. Slowly drawing it from his slacks, he methodically doubled it while staring at me. The familiar shudder ran through my body.

As he sat in the chair facing the couch, he kept the doubled belt in his hand and placed it across his lap. "I will discipline you a bit more sternly tonight…and hopefully we will get the results we both want, Miss Jensen. Do you have anything to say for yourself?"

"Uh…no…sir. I'm sorry.

"Very well, please follow me into my office." He walked ahead, the belt hanging from his hand. The room was small, crammed with books and bookshelves, just as his office at the college, and there was a table desk in the middle with a leather office chair. He pushed the pile of papers on the desk to the side, then turned and looked at me. "I want you to take your jeans down to your ankles and bend over the desk." I unbuttoned my jeans and wiggled the tight material over my hips and down my legs. Bending over the desk, I put my chest and stomach flat on the wooden surface. My legs were straight and I spread them slightly. Nothing moved in the room for a few moments and then I felt Professor Montgomery's fingers slide under the waistband of my panties. He pulled them slowly down to my ankles. I was already soaking wet, and instinctively pulled my thighs back together so he wouldn't see.

The spanking started without much pain, but the sting increased as the belt landed across my bottom with more force. Still, the delicious warm flush of my arousal, which I'm sure the sting contributed to, dominated any discomfort. He spanked me for quite a while…I was definitely being disciplined When the belt finally stopped slapping my behind…I felt the leather touch the inside of my thigh just above my knee.

"Spread your legs, Miss Jensen." I slid my feet apart as far as I could with my jeans bunched at my ankles, and knew that he could now see my soaked pussy. The leather slid slowly up my thigh until it brushed against my waiting lips. I thought I would climax…but I held on.

My spanking resumed…and continued for another couple of minutes. Hard…but not too hard. I was as turned on as I could ever remember. The belt stopped falling on my bottom once again…and then his fingers… started caressing the stinging flesh.

The cycle continued. I was spanked…then caressed. As my punishment went on, the caresses lasted longer and his fingers probed deeper between my buttocks and inside folds of my sex. My juices coated his fingers as they slid along the lips of my pussy…then he would draw them up between my cheeks and lightly across my anus.

A warm, wet sensation started to play across my bottom…circled over one cheek, then the other…slid between them, and down into my crevasse. His tongue was luxurious…it was all I could do not to explode. His hands pushed my legs farther apart and I suddenly felt the warm wetness find my clit. Flicking…sucking gently. Heaven. A few moments interruption and then I felt his dick slide up between my cheeks. I reached back and encircled it with my hands. Large…thick…softness over steel.

I pushed back and pulled him into my dripping pussy… unable to wait any longer. We fucked furiously…and exploded almost in unison.

Within a month we knew we were deeply in love. Two months later we took a weekend trip to Las Vegas and did a quickie wedding. Considering Anthony's position as a professor, and mine as his student, we felt it necessary to keep our relationship a secret until I received my undergraduate degree, so I kept my apartment and we were discreet about being seen in public.

Our relationship was bliss...perfect. We were intellectually, socially, and, of course, physically – in lockstep. Our lovemaking was extraordinary. Infatuated with each other's bodies...there wasn't a tiny millimeter, nook or crevice that we didn't explore with our tongues or fingers. For hours. There were those naughty little dildos... all sizes...for every opening...that Anthony introduced me to. His beautiful, silky smooth, thick, rock hard dick...with the scrumptious head - I could never get enough. Looking. Playing with it.. Licking and sucking it. Or having it deep inside me. Luckily, Anthony gave my pussy, ass, breasts and mouth equal attention.

He remained a firm believer in discipline, and I was punished each time he thought I needed it...or I made him think I did. He would often announce early in the day, or even the day before, that he was going to spank me...and my every waking moment until he followed through was filled with that delicious blend of anxiety, anticipation, and arousal. The spankings were long and sound enough to leave no doubt I was being punished...but never harsh. The sex that followed was even more torrid and white hot than our exquisite lovemaking sessions on the numerous occasions when I wasn't disciplined.

Other than the occasional trip out of town, we stayed isolated as a couple from others in our community. A couple of months after we were married Anthony announced that one of his best friends would be in town for a few days and we would have dinner with him. The prospect of some social interaction as a couple excited me.

Sven was a tall, slender, blond Swede, an anthropology professor and successful novelist. He and Anthony had met in graduate school, became fast friends, and decided together to remain in the US and teach. Sven's area of specialty was Native American history and culture, in particular the tribes of the great plains and southwest , and he came to his interest after being obsessed with Hollywood westerns during his youth. His two successful novels were historical fiction, built around the tragic but fascinating saga of America's early inhabitants.

Sven was a terrific conversationalist, and we had a delightful dinner at a quaint restaurant in a neighboring town. I was included in the give and take about a range of subjects, and both men seemed truly interested in my opinions. Over dessert and coffee Sven began to praise Anthony's wisdom in moving quickly to secure my hand. "Well, Tony, Judith is extraordinary. I'm even more impressed than I was sure I would be…after your glowing description. A true beauty…with a serious and quick mind. Rare, you know."

"Yes, Sven, thank you. I am indeed a lucky man…and knew it after the first couple of times I was around her." Anthony smiled warmly as he looked deep into my eyes. "Of course, she can be trying and misbehaves at times…but I've learned how to deal with that."

"And how do you deal with that?" Sven looked first at Anthony, then back as me.

"The old fashioned way. The English way. Of course. I discipline her when she needs it."

"Ah…do you?" Sven looked at me squarely. "And does she accept it?"

"Perhaps you should answer that, Judith, " Anthony said.

"Well...uh...yes. Yes, I do."

"Truth be told," Anthony said, "the fifteen minutes we had to wait on Judith while she finished getting ready... resulted in us being late for our dinner reservation. I haven't had a chance to tell her yet...but I'll have to discipline her. Tardiness is one of her recurring issues."

The shudder ran through my body.

"And when will you punish her?" Sven was looking at me when he posed the question.

"Possibility later tonight, but more likely tomorrow."

"Well, don't put if off because of me, dear friend. You know I totally agree with your approach. Perhaps it would make the lesson more pointed if I were present."

"You may be right. Interesting thought," Anthony replied.

I didn't say much on the ride home. I was tingling...a bit nervous...unsure. They discussed the state of the economy.

Anthony served night caps of Grand Marnier as we sat in the living room and discussed getting together with Sven and his wife, River. Anthony suddenly looked at me and said, "Judith, I've decided not to wait until tomorrow. I'm going to discipline you after we finish our drinks. Only fifteen minutes late, for you, is not too bad. I won't use the belt this time." My body stiffened as the current ran through it.

The drinks seemed to take forever to finish. "Judith, come here please," Anthony said as he motioned me in front of where he sat on the sofa. I stood up and moved toward him. "Pull your jeans down to your ankles and lay across my lap." My hands were sweating as I unbuttoned my skin tight jeans and began to wiggle them down over my hips. Sven was sitting in the chair to my left, at the end of the sofa. I finished pushing my pants down and then bent forward across Anthony's lap. I could feel Sven's eyes on my panty clad bottom, as he sat directly behind my legs, with a clear view. Anthony's fingers went inside the waistband of my panties and slowly pulled them down to my jeans at my ankles. I was soaking wet.

"Very well, Anthony, don't go easy on her because of me. A spanking needs to be sound to be effective."

And it was sound. With only his hand, Anthony brought a sharp sting to my bottom, but the heat of my arousal, as always, quickly took over. I wanted Sven to see, and parted my legs, arched my behind a bit higher, and wiggled it slightly after each blow.

Our lovemaking after Sven left was furious...amazing.

Shortly after I graduated, Anthony took me to a small, renovated farmhouse on five acres he had located about ten miles from town. After a walk-through we decided it was perfect. "Did you happen to notice the tool and woodshed out back, my dear?" he asked as we walked to the car.

"Yes." I smiled at him. "But what on earth do we need a woodshed for?"

I found out. For "serious misbehavior", as Anthony put it, I was marched out to the woodshed, where Anthony would take my panties down and follow through with his promise to "wear your behind out" with the strap he kept hanging on the wall. He had some bales of hay delivered, and I was told to bend over them...when I didn't have to bend over and grab my ankles. The hay also made a great place to "make up" when we were too turned on to make it back to the house.

Anthony paid $250.00 to have a fifteen foot willow tree planted in the back yard. It came with branches already long enough for a "suitable switch," and on the occasions when I was sent into the yard to fetch one...I was usually ordered into the bathroom for a switching. On other occasions I was ordered into the bedroom, where Anthony removed his belt. And for minor offenses I was turned over his lap.

A couple of months after we moved in I was introduced to what would become a once-a- month ritual; an important addition, as Anthony put it, to our "regimen of health and fitness." We worked out regularly and ate healthy meals. Of course, missing workouts or eating more than a minimum amount of junk always guaranteed that I would be disciplined...and then pleasured. I tried to be diligent.

The first time Randy and Carol arrived at our house they came through the front door lugging two portable massage tables. They were massage and holistic medicine therapists, according to their cards, and within a few minutes the tables had been set up next to each other and Anthony and I were face down and completely nude.

Randy worked on me, Carol on Anthony, and they were highly skilled at deep, therapeutic massage. Randy was a short, heavily muscled guy with blond hair and blue eyes, not at all unattractive, and in between the serious muscle work, his hands and fingers managed to lightly touch or brush across every delicate spot on my body. Massaging my breasts, his fingers flicked across my nipples. While pressing deep into the muscles of my inner thighs, they brushed lightly against my pussy. Kneading my buttocks, a finger slipped between my cheeks and flicked quickly across my anus. Hard and soft. Hard and soft. An appropriate metaphor, it suddenly occurred to me…for my desires and also my husband's skills. After soundly disciplining me, his fingers on my body were always exquisitely gentle. His tongue like velvet. Then his dick would plunge deep inside me like a piston.

From Anthony's low moans and my quick glance and glimpse of my sweetheart's gorgeous, erect and pulsating penis, I assumed Carol was working the same way. It was soothing, relaxing…and had me aroused. I doubted all their massages were this "complete". Anthony surely told them I wouldn't complain, and he was right. My perfect massage – therapeutic and erotic.

The massage was over and we were still lying on our backs when I saw the red bag and white tube in Randy's hand. His eyes were on mine as he spoke. "We've removed the toxins from your muscles, now we'll get them out of your body. Will you both please turn over"

I started to glance at Anthony, but decided to just go with the flow. Rolling over onto my stomach, I was totally still and relaxed…with a gentle current of arousal still flowing through me. I raised my head until I could see Randy's reflection in the large mirror that we had purchased to go over the mantel, but that was still propped against the wall. Watching him pull on a rubber surgical glove, I felt the heat rise in my loins. He stepped forward and I felt the cheeks of my bottom being spread…and held open. Probably for longer than necessary. His lubricated finger was cool against my anus, but the feeling was sublime as he slid it up into me...then took his time making sure I was thoroughly lubricated. After removing his finger he slowly inserted the enema tube. Watching and feeling at the same time raised my temperature even higher. The warm water felt luxurious as it flowed into me. I sighed. The overall sensation was wonderful, quietly stimulating... and I was in no hurry for it to end.

When Anthony and I emerged from the bathrooms Randy and Carol and all their equipment were gone. Excellent timing...since we couldn't wait to attack and devour each other's bodies and ended up on the carpet in the living room, making wild, wanton love.

In the Fall Sven and his wife River came for a weekend visit. The moment I opened the door and they walked into our home I was mesmerized. And Sven's story crystallized.

River was a full blooded Native American, and one of the most stunning women I had ever seen. High cheekbones, jet black hair, perfect features on a broad face with an exquisite, light copper complexion. Her body was amazing. Full breasts with plenty of cleavage on display above the knot in her cinched halter, with enough natural sag to indicate God's hand. A tiny waist and flat stomach, flowing into full, round hips and buttocks that were on clear display in tight, cotton shorts molded to each cheek. As she walked, each full, round orb jutted back...then forward...like pistons. Her solid, muscular thighs tapering to perfectly sculpted calves, tapering to tiny ankles, completed her goddess body. Defined muscle mass from genetics and the gym, overlaid by a layer of smooth feminine curves and softness. Exactly what I was sure was every man's true dream. My looks and body rarely made me envious of other women. With River, I was.

She was a doll, though, and after an animated introduction and hour of conversation between us, we took off for a consignment clothing shop a few miles away that was a favorite of mine, leaving the men to man the grill and the tenderloin. River was quite the shopper, and we made a few other stops. We knew we were late on the drive home, but nothing much was said about it. I wondered.

I opened the door to confront Sven and Anthony staring at us...sternly. Sven spoke immediately. "I assume this was your fault, River. Never found a shop you could leave in a timely manner. We made it very clear that the tenderloin would be ready at 7:00. It's either cold, or overdone...or both." River didn't speak, and neither did I. Sven continued, in a calm, but steely voice. "Did you notice the quaint little woodshed when we came in?" I felt my stomach tighten and a tingle flash through my body.

"Yes, Sven." River's voice was calm.

"After dinner," he stared at her as he spoke, then slowly started to unbuckle the leather belt he wore, "I'm going to take you to our host's woodshed." Pulling it from his trousers, then doubling it in his hand, he continued, "And I'm going to use my belt on your behind."

I quickly looked at Anthony. He glanced at me but said nothing.

Sven placed the belt on the corner of the table beside his plate and left it there during dinner. At first the table was a bit quiet, but by the time the slightly overcooked entrée arrived, conversation had resumed at full speed for the other three. My mind was racing too much to concentrate very long on the discussions of politics and exotic vacation spots. I kept glancing at the belt...and was acutely aware of the dampness in my panties.

"River, follow me please," Swen said, standing up and pushing back his chair after we had finished dessert. "It's time for your trip to the woodshed."

I glanced at Anthony. He too rose, then started to unbuckle his belt. "You were complicit, Judith. You knew what time it was. I'm going to tan your bottom as soon as Sven is finished with River."

Quite a revealing procession. River, followed by me, headed across the short expanse of yard toward the woodshed. Sven and Anthony just behind us, each with a belt hanging from his hand. Once inside Sven spoke. "River, pull your shorts down, step out of them, and turn around."

She did as she was told, and her blue, sheer, clinging panties only partially covered her magnificent bottom. Sven stepped forward and pulled her panties down to her ankles. I was dripping wet...and not sure if it was due to the prospect of watching River get a spanking or the mere sight of her body. The skin on her bottom was unblemished and a slightly lighter shade of light copper. Her buttocks were two separate, highly defined, firm, round globes, flowing into her beautiful legs. Sven told her to bend forward and grab her ankles. As she did as she was told, she spread her legs slightly. Her bottom was so full that even arched and spread as she bent over her cheeks did not part enough for a glimpse between them. But the jet black hair between her legs and the bright pink, glistening lips of her pussy were clearly visible.

River began wriggling her bottom and squirming shortly after Sven began spanking her with his belt. Her hips were very active, and the sight of her beautiful bottom turning pink and glimpses of her pussy were delicious. The spanking was definitely thorough, but in no way severe. When it was over Sven told her to leave her panties around her ankles while I was punished.

"All right, Judith, take your shorts off." I did as I was told. Standing still in only my panties and short, tight top, I felt fingers slip inside the waistband and my panties were slowly lowered, then removed, from behind. "Bend over and grab your ankles and spread your legs." Again I followed orders. I was into it…anxious…turned on…about to get a spanking in front of River and Sven. I knew they were turned on. Anthony started…and spanked me a bit harder than usual. No doubt to impress our guests. The sting was significant as his belt slapped across my bottom again and again. I gave in to abandon…writhed, moaned, and spread my legs farther apart. Knowing they had a clear view of the intimate details of my behind and pussy as I squirmed and arched my bottom, I was pushed to a brief, shuddering orgasm. The rebound was fast. A couple of more slaps with the belt and I was again frantic with excitement and lust. An image flashed through my mind of the awesome lovemaking Anthony and I would do later – his tongue tickling my clit, a finger brushing over my nipples, another slipping into my bottom, his steel-hard cock filling me. A multiple orgasm night. Maybe three or four. Life couldn't be better!

Camp Counselor

"Lake at Camp Cherokee to close due to toxic levels."

The headline took me back thirty years in a millisecond, to that midnight and Will Champion.

I was seventeen and in my first year as a senior camp counselor at Camp Cherokee after spending two summers as a junior counselor. As soon as all the girls in my cabin were safely tucked in for the 10:00 p.m. curfew and the lights were out, I moved stealthily down the path to the boathouse to meet Billy Laughlin.

We spent a couple of hours hidden between racks of Old Town canoes, drinking from Billy's bottle of bourbon and smoking cigarettes. We kissed more than a few times and I let him rub my breast inside my bra. At midnight I knew I was pushing my luck, Billy was becoming more aggressive, so I abruptly left.

I had walked about a hundred yards of the quarter mile from the boathouse to the cabin when a voice from the dark made me jump and gasp. "Out kinda late, aren't you Lisa?" Will Champion was sitting on one of the ancient wooden benches along the path. "You look a little shaky."

Will was the camp god. An all state football player, he was spending the last of five summers at Cherokee, before going off to the University of Maryland on a full scholarship. He supervised all the counselors, all activities, and reported directly to Mr. Spruill, the camp director. There were four senior girl counselors in camp, and as far as I knew every one of us had a world class crush on Will. Big, terrific body, handsome as an actor, with curly blond hair and the best tan around. The scoop was he wasn't too bright, but what did that matter at my age and with everything else he had going.

"Uh…wh…what are you doing here?" My voice was a squeak as my breath was still caught in my throat.

"Just got finished with a run." He stood up, took a couple of steps forward, and towered over me. "I can smell it, Lisa. Liquor and cigarettes. Where have you been and who were you with?"

"I…I haven't been…wh…with anyone. Just for a walk."

"Come on, Lisa. Don't make it worse. I have an obligation. This will get you kicked out of camp."

"I'm so sorry." I started crying. "I just had a little bit."

"Who were you with?"

"Oh…please…please." My mind was madly spinning…trying to think what to say.

"Who?"

"Billy. But we didn't do anything. We were just talking."

"You'll have to meet with Mr. Spruill tomorrow. I'm sorry but he just doesn't tolerate this kind of behavior. Let's see…out past curfew, drinking, smoking…Billy probably copped a couple of feels too."

"Please don't, Will. I promise I'll make it up. I'm so, so sorry."

He looked at me for a long moment, let his eyes wander down to my camp gym shorts and legs. "You really messed up, didn't you?"

"Uh...Yeah. I did."

"Don't you think you deserve to be punished?"

"I...I guess so. Yes."

"Well, what do you suggest? It's not like I can ground you around here. If I mention anything...and the honor code in camp means I should...it will all come out." He stared at me for another long moment. "You were in the boathouse, right?"

"Yeah."

"OK, here's the deal. You meet me at 11:00 tomorrow night in the boathouse and I'll give you a good, old fashioned spanking. And I'll let it go at that."

"No. I mean..."

"You deserve to be punished, Lisa. You admit it. I can't just let you off. This is the only way I can figure to keep you from getting kicked out of camp, and still get punished for what you did." Another long pause. He was staring down, directly at me. I was staring at my feet.

"OK." I turned and walked very quickly up the path.

I didn't fall asleep for hours. When I opened my eyes the next morning thoughts and images exploded through my mind. It wasn't a dream. It really happened.

I went through my counselor duties in a fog. Kids had

to repeat themselves…all day. I was present in body only. A real space cadet. Was I really going to let Will Champion give me a spanking? I've got a date with the camp… hell…the state…hunk. I'm going to be with him in a remote boathouse…with no one else around. But it's only because he's going to punish me. I was scared… mortified…but there was something else. Sneaking out with Will Champion…for any reason. I felt a curious tingle…knowing he was going to *do something intimate to me*. And even at my still tender age…I imagined there were a few possibilities.

The most painful thoughts were trying to imagine what he would actually do. I had never been spanked, but when I visited my cousins and aunt on the farm, Mary Jo would sometimes mention the spankings her stepfather gave her and her brother. I suddenly remembered her puzzling smile when she told me he would send her to get a switch from a tree in the backyard, take her into the barn, and then make her pull down her jeans and panties and bend over for a switching. Surely Will wouldn't…

It was an incredibly long day. I did everything I could to avoid Will Champion. On two occasions I didn't. My head stayed down and he ignored me. By ten o'clock, when I turned the lights off in my cabin, I was a nervous wreck. But there was still that other, confusing, *something else*. I had tried more than a few times during the day to formulate a speech that would make him change his mind, but something told me I didn't want him to just say OK and walk away. Or did I?

I put on a clean pair of my high school volleyball team sweat pants, a camp T shirt, tennis shoes and white socks, some perfume, and combed my hair as best as I could with trembling hands. I constantly looked around for any sign of life as I walked down the path, then through the door into the boat house.

"Over here, Lisa." I heard his voice before I could see him, hidden between the last row of canoes and the side wall of the boathouse. I moved around the rows of boats and was in front of Will, seated on a wood bench.

"Please remember, Lisa, I am doing you a favor." His voice seemed a bit weak. I remember thinking he looked nervous. "It's the only way I can think of to keep you from getting kicked out of camp." I thought, in a flash, *not an option in my family.* "You've got to swear you won't tell anyone about this."

"Okay."

"Pull your sweat pants down."

I couldn't believe I was doing it, but it was as if my hands were somehow directly controlled by his voice. I undid the tie, then quickly slipped them down to my ankles. His eyes dropped to my waist and legs...and lingered.

"Now, lay across my lap."

Again, I didn't hesitate. The bench was low, and my face ended up just above the floor. He shifted my hips until my bottom was arched across his thighs, which were steel hard through his jeans. I could also feel his penis...it was hard.

"Be as quiet as possible, okay?"

I didn't say anything. Then I felt his fingers under the waistband of my panties. "Don't." I tried to reach back and grab his hand. He firmly grasped my wrist. "Please...

don't."

"I told you", he said, with a firm voice now, "I'm going to give you a sound spanking. Don't make me change my mind. We can still go to Mr. Spruill's office"

I remember the feel of the cool night air against the skin of my bottom as he pulled my panties down to my ankles. Nothing happened. I could hear his breathing…loud and uneven. The first couple of blows felt very soft. Was this it? He started spanking me harder, but it still didn't hurt. Only a slight sting that, surprisingly, began to feel good. There were long pauses between spanks. Then I felt his hand on my behind, gently rubbing, caressing. I was excited…my breathing changed…became louder. That familiar stirring in my loins whenever I was turned on was there. The tingling grew stronger as his hand slipped between my thighs and lightly brushed the lips of my pussy. A momentary twinge of embarrassment flashed through me as I wondered if I was wet. I spread my legs a bit. His fingers brushed over my lips again…and again. They slid up along my behind and then he pushed them down between my cheeks. A shudder ran through my body.

He started spanking me again, and I think it was harder. But 95% of my being was consumed by the lust that had exploded through me. I only remember pleasure.

He stopped the spanking again. His fingers caressed me again. They slid deeper into my pussy. And stayed longer between my buttocks. I couldn't help myself. I was moaning.

"Stand up, Lisa." The words jolted me from my state of rapture.

I did as he said. Will got up form the bench and I remember desperately wanting to unzip his pants and release his penis, which was clearly visible as a large lump in his jeans. He unbuckled his belt and pulled it from his jeans.

"Now, bend over that canoe", he said, as he motioned to the boat turned upside down across two sawhorses.

I took a couple of steps, my sweats and panties still at my ankles, and bent forward. All I could think of was being touched again. God, I wanted him to do *something* else to me.

I looked back and he had the belt in his hand. He began to spank me, but again, the blows weren't heavy...and the sting and slap of the leather against my skin seemed to stoke my lust even higher. The spanking stopped...and then I felt the leather slide between my legs and brush against my pussy. I instinctively parted my legs. The belt slid very gently along my lips. I was dripping. The cool leather slipped up between my cheeks and I could feel it brush across my tiny opening. My moans, I knew, were too loud.

Suddenly I felt the weight of his body against mine. He was kissing the back of my neck, my shoulders, then turned my head and covered my mouth with his. His hot tongue felt frantic. There were a couple of long kisses, then he stood up and within seconds I felt his tongue sliding down my back...lower...between the cheeks of my behind...and then to my pussy.

I had started having sex a year earlier, when I was sixteen, with my boyfriend. But I had never felt anything like this...the waves of ecstasy that flowed through me.

When Will's penis suddenly pushed in and filled my pussy from behind, we started fucking like animals, and if the boathouse had not been so remote...we would have both been kicked out of camp...or worse.

After all these years I still vividly remember that strange mix of fear, embarrassment and lust. And the strange allure of the feel of the leather slapping against the skin of my bare bottom, so close to those *special* places that still drive me crazy...with attention from the right person. A real shame...that so many people think a 46 year old lady is too old to be spanked.

Training and Enlightenment

A curious, nervous, unsettling silence fills the inside of the BMW considering that each of the four travelers normally has to fight for an opening to get in half of what they want to say.

Well, perhaps not so curious, Sandy thinks. It's been over thirty minutes since they left, and that means in less than fifteen more she will be dropped off at a house none of them have ever been to, filled with people none of them have ever met, where she will undergo a weekend of, as Gregory put it...'fairly intense sexual reprogramming, erotic training and constructive discipline.'

It started about a month ago. She recalls their having finished dinner with Mark and Donna, still sitting at the table polishing off the last of the second or third bottle of good Merlot. The conversation was beginning to angle toward one of their regular little B&D foursomes when Gregory began to hit on her especially hard about not doing her share around the house, becoming less sexually aggressive, and, in general, acting like a world class bitch.

Convinced he was going beyond the normal 'don't you guys think she needs to be punished to straighten her out' scenario, Sandy brought the full force of her defensiveness, stinging sarcasm, and bravado down on him, while suggesting she was domestically and sexually perfect.

114

Gregory responded by mentioning a place he had casually brought up a few months before at another one of their gatherings...a place that 'provides sexual training and enlightenment'. A place, according to him, she could never handle, because she plays the role of being perfect to hide her inadequacies, and is far too insecure and cowardly to try anything that might be enough of a challenge to really have an effect on her. He went on to say it was a shame she couldn't handle it, because in addition to the corrective and educational benefits, the place was supposed to be a truly great sexual adventure - for the open-minded.

Speaking before she thought, as is often her curse, Sandy reiterated that she was the last person to need sexual training, that her courage was twice his, and she would love the opportunity for the adventure. Damned right she'd go. Where is this place and how soon could she get there?

Well, she'll be getting there in less than ten minutes by her latest, clandestine peak at her watch. Her palms are suddenly sweaty. She hasn't learned that much more about the place since she committed to going. Its reputation is impeccable, and absolutely no real harm will come to her. They had checked that out carefully. The 'real' next to the "harm" is the word that bothers her. Put that into the context of 'constructive discipline,' another of the terms she heard over the phone, and it's certainly food for thought. She and Gregory have been into B&D for a couple of years. They have their sessions with Mark and Donna, but those are mostly just spankings with, occasionally, some mild bondage thrown in. Gregory has spanked her fairly hard with his belt a couple of times, and it turned her on, or at least didn't turn her off...but then what is hard? She recalls the day he came home with the razor strap from the antique store and they set off for the country and found the deserted farmhouse. He made a production out of marching her out to the woodshed in the back, strap hanging from his hand. One car slowed; likely to watch this time-honored procession endured in various states of angst or outright panic by many thousands of boys and girls of rural America. She remembers her bottom being a little sensitive on the ride home, but doesn't remember much else about the 'trip to the woodshed' because she was focused on the spiders she could see while bending over, her shorts and panties at her knees, holding her ankles. What she does remember is their frantic lovemaking in the long, cool grass just in back of the shed.

"Well, here we are. Cat seems to have had your tongue for the last few minutes, Dear; but of course knowing you I realize it couldn't be nerves. Have a wonderful time Dear. I can't wait to get you back home Sunday night and see the new you."

"I can promise you it will be the old me, Gregory, with one more experience under my belt that you'll be jealous of as soon as I tell you about it."

"I hope you enjoy it," Donna says, rather sheepishly.

"Me, too," says Mark, with more conviction. "I wish I were going, sounds like great fun. I'd at least like to watch."

They turn into a drive and are stopped by a closed, weathered, heavy wooden gate set between two stone columns.

"You better get out and tell them who you are, Dear", Gregory says, "try ringing that button next to the speaker box."

Sandy steps from the car and feels her knees shaking as she approaches the box. *God, and I'm not even to the door yet. Calm down. This is going to be fun, remember that.*

She pushes the button and waits.

"Can I help you"? A voice, feminine and aristocratic, comes through the box.

"I'm Sandy Howard. I'm here for the weekend."

"Yes, Mrs. Howard. Please drive in and then come to the door alone. The door will not be opened until the automobile has passed back through the gate and departed the premises."

She walks back to the car, opens the front door and sits down. The gate swings open.

"Drive in and then let me off. They said you have to leave before they will let me in."

"Ah, such wonderful intrigue. You're going to love it, dear, but I would be on my best behavior if I were you. These people just might be slightly less indulgent of your wise ass attitude than I am."

"Fuck you all. Let me out of here so I can get on with a great weekend of sex while you rush home to watch the football game".

The house is large, of weathered clapboards, with the main section resembling a huge barn with its nine-paneled roof - not atypical of the numerous country estates found in this part of New England. She doesn't bother with any additional good-byes when the car stops in the circular, gravel driveway in front of the door, and quickly grabs the small bag containing only toiletries and makeup: exactly what she was instructed to bring with her. She swings the car door open and quickly steps out on the walkway to the front entrance. As she arrives in front of the door she is aware she has not heard the car leave. She turns, stares, and is met with one of Gregory's maddening little mocking smiles and waves as he leans over and his face fills the passenger window. The car begins to move away and she turns back and reaches for the button to the right of the door. She is again aware of moisture on her palms and unsteadiness in her knees. She tries to clear her voice but even the cough doesn't come out very strong. Pushing the button, she waits, then glances down at the tight, black leather skirt which ends well above her knees, the matching vest and white, form fitting blouse, cut low over her breasts, and the high heels - all of which Gregory insisted that she wear. She wishes she had worn the more conservative long dress and stockings that she had considered. But again, she couldn't show any signs of concern or lack of boldness.

The door opens and a tall, elegant woman appearing to be in her late thirties is behind it. "Come in, please, follow me."

The voice sounds the same, minus the electronic embellishment, as the one that came through the speaker. As Sandy follows her down a long hall she notices the woman is dressed in a dark suit with long skirt and puffy, padded shoulders. She tugs on her own skirt as she walks, trying to pull it lower.

They come to an open door on the left and the woman motions for her to enter. The room looks like a library, with rich, cherry judges paneling, filled bookcases, oriental rugs and a large, ornate writing table with an inlaid leather top. There are two corduroy wing chairs on either side of a floor lamp against one wall and a leather sofa and coffee table against another.

The woman leads her to the sofa and tells her to sit. She lifts a leather portfolio off of the table and hands it to her.

"Fill out the first two pages and nothing more. Do not look beyond the first two pages," she says, rather firmly, then turns and walks back into the hall.

Sandy opens the folder to see that the first page is the standard name and address, personal and family particulars. The second page is filled with questions regarding medical history and current problems, prescription drugs, substance abuse, and psychological problems such as phobias, and treatments.

She fills out the two pages, and then, glancing up to be sure no one is looking into the room through a door, quickly turns the page. There are more detailed physical and medically related statistics such as height, weight, blood pressure and temperature on the third page, and she sees the next has a series of questions relating to sexual practices and fantasies. She begins to read, her attention riveted by the descriptive wording.

"Do not close the folder or attempt to turn the page Mrs. Howard."

She looks up, startled, to see a very distinguished looking middle-aged man standing by the writing table, staring at her. Tall and trim, his dark skin is set against swept back graying hair and a neat mustache. A double-breasted navy blazer with a paisley silk ascot add to his elegance and fit well with his clipped, aristocratic accent. French, she guesses. He walks forward, his eyes still riveted on hers, and takes the portfolio from her hands. Turning, he goes around the writing table, pulls the wingback, tufted leather chair out, and sits down.

"Mrs. Howard, you don't follow directions particularly well, do you?"

She doesn't know what to say, so says nothing.

"We're not getting off to a very good start, my dear. Now, I want you to answer me when I ask you the question again. My name is Mr. Lancaster and you will always address me as either Mr. Lancaster or Sir. Is that clear?"

"Yes Mr. Lancaster."

"You do not follow directions particularly well, do you?"

"No, but I didn't mean..."

"You are not answering me as I asked you to. No what? Mrs. Howard?"

"No sir," she says, shaken now to the point that her voice is weak and unsteady.

"Very well, Mrs. Howard. Stand up and move to the middle of the room and face me."

She does as he asks, nervously twirling her thumbs together in front of her.

"Stand straight, Mrs. Howard, and put your hands down by your side."

His eyes quickly examine her. Reasonably tall, with

long, neat, shapely legs tapering up to her short skirt, a fine, small waist, and what from the front appear to be full, rounded hips. Jutting breasts with nipples that look erect show through her blouse, and she has a lovely, girlish, narrow face with sparkling, almond-shaped green eyes, an aquiline nose, and a stunning shock of thick, wavy, luxurious red hair that falls over her shoulders. *Very nice indeed.*

"Mrs. Howard, you are now at the Center For Personal Enlightenment, Training, and Correction. You have come here to improve your personal responsiveness, actions, and attitudes in your relationship with your husband, a Mr. Gregory Howard. Is that correct?"

"Yes, Mr. Lancaster."

"That's much better, Mrs. Howard."

"You've come here of your own free will. Is that correct, Mrs. Howard?"

"Yes, Mr. Lancaster."

"Mrs. Howard, the emphasis here is on personal training and development. Personal, in our vernacular, refers to matters that are sexual. Our goal is to have you leave here a much more imaginative, creative, responsive, and aggressive person in your sexual relationship with your husband, or anyone else with whom you might become involved. In order for you to get the maximum benefit from the next two days and nights it is imperative that you do exactly as you are told, and do it the instant you are told, with absolutely no questions or signs of reluctance on your part. Do you understand what I have just told you, Mrs. Howard?"

"Yes, Mr. Lancaster."

"An example of what we will not tolerate here is the total disregard for the instructions you were given regarding the paperwork you were asked to fill out, and the disrespect you showed in the way you addressed me with your initial answers to my questions. Do you understand this?"

"Yes, Mr. Lancaster."

"Although we prefer to keep the emphasis on training and development, there will be correction involved. How much, Mrs. Howard, will be up to you. By correction we are referring to corrective measures, or discipline if you will, that will help you attain the maximum benefit from the time you spend with us. Did you know that there would be discipline involved in your stay with us.

"Yes, but..."

"Yes, what?, Mrs. Howard." His voice takes on a much sharper tone.

She feels herself becoming flustered again, lowers head to avoid his stare and looks at the floor. "Yes, Mr. Lancaster."

"Look at me, Mrs. Howard. Do not ever look away from me or anyone here when they are speaking to you. Is that understood?"

"Yes, Mr. Lancaster."

"All of the discipline here, with a very few exceptions, takes the form of corporal punishment. What does the phrase corporal punishment mean to you, Mrs. Howard?"

"Uh, it means, uh, physical punishment."

There is a pause as he stares even more intently at her; she feels as if his eyes are penetrating her skull.

"Mrs. Howard, you are again not doing well. You will, I assure you, be on very intimate and familiar terms with our methods of corrective discipline if you can not even follow directions as simple as how to address me."

"Yes, Mr. Lancaster. I'm sorry, Mr. Lancaster." She realizes her control is slipping, and feels the first sign of moisture in her eyes. Suddenly considering turning and running for the door, she quickly shifts her thoughts to calming herself. She knows she can handle this and determines to stay cool, meet this guy head on.

"Now, once again, what does corporal punishment mean to you, Mrs. Howard."

"It means physical punishment, Mr. Lancaster."

"And what types of physical discipline do you think of when you hear the phrase corporal punishment?"

"Uh, spanking, uh,....spankings, Mr. Lancaster."

"Very good. Whenever there is a need for corrective, disciplinary measures here, almost without exception, some form of spanking is used. Does your husband spank you, Mrs. Howard?"

"Uh, sometimes, uh yes, Mr. Lancaster."

"And does he spank you to discipline you or as foreplay?"

"Mostly foreplay, I guess, Mr. Lancaster."

"The two reasons do not have to be exclusive, Mrs. Howard, but there is a difference," he says as he gives her just a hint of a smile and a raised eyebrow.

She is suddenly aware that her palms are sweating and her leather skirt is wet where she has had them pressed tightly against it.

"How many times we have to discipline you is of your choosing, Mrs. Howard. We operate on a demerit system here. The discipline can be meted out as soon as the demerits are assigned, or they can be held over and accumulated. It is totally up to the staff member that assigns you the demerits. Your file will be completely reviewed by myself three times each day and any unresolved demerits will be dealt with. When you have received five demerits you will be spanked or paddled. Ten and someone will take a belt or strap to your bottom. Fifteen and…well…somewhat harsher punishments will be your reward. Any member of the staff is empowered to determine and carry out discipline. "Do you understand everything that I have just told you, Mrs. Howard?"

"Yes, Mr. Lancaster."

"We, of course, will do nothing that will injure you or cause you any real harm. However, there definitely is a difference in constructive discipline and foreplay."

He pauses for a moment, his stare again seems to intensify, and she recognizes the phrase that had bothered her before she came. She feels her face flush.

"I will only repeat this one more time, Mrs. Howard. The amount of discipline you require will be determined solely by your actions. There is only one punishment that has been mandated by your recent unresponsiveness toward your husband. That will be in the form of a thorough spanking that you will receive later this evening. The rest is up to you."

Sandy feels a lump in her throat, cotton in her mouth.

"I do so hope you will cooperate to the best of your ability, as this can be a very illuminating and enjoyable weekend for you, and one that will lead to years of increased pleasure. You must, of course, now sign this consent form that attests to the fact that you understand everything I have told you and that you are staying here of your own free will."

Again she feels the urge to turn and leave....even starts to tell him, catches herself. *I'm tough, can't cop out. It's going to be fun.*

She walks forward and signs the sheet of paper after pretending to read it, but without trying.

"Very well, Mrs. Howard, the first thing we must do is document your physical condition. Please follow Miss Quinley."

Sandy hears the door open the instant Mr. Lancaster has finished speaking, and as she turns she faces the woman who showed her in.

"Follow me, please." The voice is crisp, and the person she now knows as Miss Quinley leads her down the hall. She walks fast to keep up with the quick pace and after they turn a corner a door to the right is opened for her and she is ushered in.

It is a small room, with an examination table in the middle. "Take off all of your clothes, fold them neatly and lay them on the chair, and have a seat on the table." Miss Quinley says, then turns abruptly and walks out, closing the door behind her.

Sandy looks around at the white walls and gray tile floor of the drab room, with its collection of cabinets, trays, a scale, an eye chart - all reminders of every doctor's office she has seen. She notices the T-shaped floor stand in the corner with the red bag and curled white tube hanging from it, and feels a quick shudder. Suddenly remembering what she was told to do, she pulls off her jacket and starts to take off her blouse so quickly that she fumbles with the buttons. She unzips the tight skirt, steps out of it, and wonders if she should keep on the high cut, black lace panties. She recalls being told to fold her clothes, and she hurries to gather them and place them on the chair. She sits on the examination table and is thinking about her panties again when the door suddenly opens and Mr. Lancaster and a beautiful young man with a white lab coat walk in.

He appears to be no more than twenty-five, is tall and slender, has a perfect, rosy complexion, extraordinary, sharp, exquisite features, and thick, darkish blond hair worn in the current style, with the sides trimmed close. She is startled and transfixed by his looks

"Mrs. Howard," the voice of Mr. Lancaster jolts her, "this is Mr. Rawls. He is our physician's assistant and will be conducting your examination. I see that you have been negligent in following directions again, Mrs. Howard."

She feels the heat come back to her face. "I thought I did what I was told, Mr. Lancaster."

"You thought, Mrs. Howard. Perhaps you didn't listen correctly. We'll soon find out."

She sees him touch a device that looks like a beeper on

his trousers. She thinks about pulling the panties off quickly, doesn't, and then sees Miss Quinley walk into the room.

"Miss. Quinley, did you tell Mrs. Howard to take off all her clothes?"

"Yes, Mr. Lancaster, I did."

"Thank you, Miss Quinley." She turns and disappears into the hall.

"Mrs. Howard, why did you not take off all your clothes as you were instructed?"

"I'm sorry," Mr. Lancaster. She reaches for the waistband, starts to push her panties down as he speaks again.

"Leave them on for now, Mrs. Howard. I want you to look down at them until I tell you to look up. Perhaps that will help you remember to pay attention to what you are told."

"Go over to the scale, please, Mrs. Howard." Rawls voice is soft and flat.

She slides off the table.

"Keep looking at your panties, Mrs. Howard. I do not want you to forget."

"Step up please." Rawls says as he moves toward her and she notices the portfolio in his hands. He adjusts the weights. "One hundred twenty two." He raises the bar so he can measure her height. "Five feet six. Please step down and go back to the table and lay on your stomach."

Lancaster gazes at the smallish, yet perfect, rounded

breasts with tiny, erect nipples, hanging ever so slightly and moving rhythmically as she crosses the floor. Her waist is tiny and her hips and buttocks even more shapely spilling out of the tight, high-cut panties than they had appeared under her clothes in his office.

Sandy can see Rawls open a cabinet to the side of her as she lays on her stomach with her face turned to the side. Slowly pulling on a rubber glove, he removes what appears to be a tube of KY lubricant, takes off the top, and places it on the counter. He then opens a drawer and steps in front of it. When he turns back she sees he is shaking a thermometer.

"Mrs. Howard, I'm going to take your temperature." He pulls up the stool and sits with his beautiful head not more than a foot from hers. He looks straight into her eyes and speaks in an even softer voice now, just as flat. "This is a rectal thermometer, so will you please pull your panties down for me."

She is stunned for a moment, can't move, then quickly reaches back for her panties and begins to turn onto her side and draw her legs up to slide them off.

"Stay as you are, Mrs. Howard," comes Lancaster's stern voice. "Remain on your stomach. You can get them down that way. And I want them all the way to your knees. Perhaps it would have been easier if you had followed your instructions."

She buries her face in the paper sheet on the table and pushes until the panties are just below her buttocks. She cannot reach any farther and starts to twist her body again.

Lancaster marvels at the beautiful, smooth curves of her

exposed ass...full, milk white, and firm. "Do not change your position, Mrs. Howard. I believe if you will arch and raise your buttocks you can accomplish what you need to."

She slowly lifts her hips, and then, realizing it's not enough, thrusts her bottom higher into the air as she draws her knees up towards her. She feels her thighs part and the cheeks of her bottom open slightly, and the eyes on them, as she wriggles and struggles, excruciatingly embarrassed, until the panties are finally at her knees. She quickly flattens her stomach back on the table.

There is moisture in her eyes again, and after a few moments she feels the touch of fingers on her bottom and then cool air on her most intimate opening as her cheeks are spread and held wide apart.

The small, pink, hairless bud of her anus is now clearly visible to Lancaster, and he moves forward to within inches of the end of the table.

"Please relax, Mrs. Howard," Rawls says, as he massages the lubricant into her tiny hole with his finger. She then she feels the cool, hard thermometer sliding into her rectum.

After what seems far longer than the normal three minutes it is removed and she is told to sit up. Rawls looks into her eyes with the pinpoint light, checks her heartbeat with a stethoscope and then begins a slow examination of her breasts. His touch is gentle and the soft kneading of his fingers causes the first faint stirrings of arousal to begin to meld with her anxiety and embarrassment. The examination lingers on her nipples, and by the time she is laying on her back and he has moved his pressing motion from her stomach to her lower abdomen, with his fingers lightly brushing through her pubic hair, the warm stirring in her loins is more than faint.

He pulls her panties the rest of the way off, places his hands just below her knees, and, again staring into her eyes, begins to lift her legs. "I need you to spread your legs for me now, Mrs. Howard. And hold them apart"

Lancaster watches the perfect triangle of untrimmed reddish hair angle down to the glistening pink petals of her sex as her thighs unfold. At the end of the table, Rawls pulls on another rubber glove.

Any doubts she has about how wet she has become are answered as Rawls finger slides smoothly from the bottom of her lips upward. She is sure there are two fingers that enter her and probe gently. After a moment they are removed and then she feels them trace up the lips again, and back down, and up, then touch the little engorged bead, linger, slide deep into her and back out. It is all she can do to keep from gasping. As he continues to massage the tiny spot, slowly, she presses her eyes tightly together and hopes she doesn't cum.

The fingers are suddenly pulled away.

"Please stand down, Mrs. Howard." Rawls voice is crisper now.

Shaken from her state of bliss, she closes her legs and slides off the table, standing in front of the two men with her hands together, trying to hide her triangle of pubic hair and what she knows are her glistening folds.

"Please bend forward over the end of the table, with your chest flat against it."

Sandy does as she is told.

"Spread the cheeks of your bottom for me, Mrs. Howard"

She hesitates.

"Do as you are told, now," comes the command from Lancaster.

She reaches back, grabs her bottom with her hands and, very tentatively, pulls the globes apart.

"Farther apart, Mrs. Howard."

As she holds her buttocks open, bent over, her feelings are confused. She is ashamed and angry at the humiliating examination, wants to cry, or scream at them, but is too frightened not to obey. And there is also the tingling warmth of arousal seeping through her. Rawls moves directly into her line of sight, and very methodically, slowly, slides the rubber glove off and replaces it with another. He steps behind her and she soon feels a lubricated finger push against her anus, then slide up into her. There is the sensation of her ass being filled, the finger starts moving, twisting, slowly, and the delicious tingling intensifies. She wants to reach down and touch herself, wants him to touch her, and unconsciously tries to lift herself to him. She feels the gentle circling motion against her clit again, and is quickly back to the peak of arousal. This time she moans before she can catch herself, and thinks about giving in.

The finger slides slowly out.

"All right, Mrs. Howard, sit back on the table please." Rawls voice is again crisp.

As she straightens up and turns she sees that Miss Quinley is now in the room and holding some clothes and a pair of white high heels in her hands. Sitting back on the table, she tries to control her breathing, tries to synchronize her body with her mind.

"Mrs. Howard, you have earned five demerits for your refusal to follow Miss Quigley's instructions to remove all of your clothes for this examination, and another five for not following the instructions she gave you regarding your portfolio when you first arrived. There is normally one more procedure for you associated with your physical exam, but we'll delay that. Miss Quinley, would you care to discipline her now?"

Sandy feels her face grow warm again as the tall, statuesque woman stares into her eyes with a slight, haughty smile, then looks her up and down. She walks past her and she can hear one of the drawers of the cabinet open. When Miss Quinley reappears in front of her she is holding a short handled, wooden hairbrush in her right hand, resting it in her left. Again she looks at Sandy without speaking. Sandy drops her eyes.

"Do not look away from her, Mrs. Howard," Lancaster says.

"Have you had a spanking since you've been here, my dear?"

"No, Miss Quinley."

"Stand down, please."

Sandy quickly steps off the table and faces the three of them.

"Put your hands down by your side," Miss Quinley says as she pulls the straight back chair over from against the wall and sits down in it.

She takes Sandy's hand and pulls her around so that her back is toward the two men, and Lancaster and Rawls eyes now feast on the head of thick, strawberry blond hair cascading down to the lovely hourglass figure and heart-shaped bottom; the white, slightly plump globes exquisitely smooth and firm.

"Now I want you to lay across my lap, Mrs. Howard."

Sandy leans down and drops her head to just above the floor, her hands touching it, her buttocks jutting upward in a perfectly rounded arc across the woman's thighs, her legs slightly apart, the thatch of hair between her thighs clearly visible to the two men.

"Mr. Lancaster, does she have any further punishment scheduled?"

"Yes, I will discipline her later this evening."

"Then I will only take five demerits from her forgetful behind right now. I'll save the hairbrush, or the strap, for another time."

Sandy sees the hairbrush drop to the floor and then feels the first sharp sting of the woman's open palm. The second blow comes a few moments later, the next a few after that and then the speed and strength of her hand increases dramatically. The spanking is short, but in Sandy's view, hard, and before it ends there is moisture in her eyes and she is kicking her legs and squirming to try to protect her burning behind. When it stops she feels the woman's fingers gently caressing her cheeks, moving slowly up and down her crack, then brushing the lips of her sex. The heat from the caresses begins to take precedence over the sting from the spanking, and the two together cause her to feel the arousal and wetness return.

"You may get up now, Mrs. Howard," Miss Quinley says.

She hears the door close. When she stands she sees Rawls and Lancaster have left.

"You must wear these at all times unless you are told not to." Quinley hands her the white silk garments and white high heels. The pants should always be pulled high enough for you to feel the material against the lips of your pussy. Dress quickly now."

She puts on the thin, high cut, white silk tap pants and matching top. When she has pulled them up as she was told, the voluptuous, pink-tinged cheeks of her ass jut from below the material, which clings to the full, round globes, the seam buried so deeply between them that it presses against her anus. Her breasts cause the top to stand out from her body, as it is so short it barely covers them. She bends over to put on the heels and is conscious of her breasts hanging beneath the blouse.

"Follow me, please."

Sandy walks behind Quinley back into the hall and again she is ushered into Lancaster's office. He is seated behind the desk and doesn't acknowledge them. Quinley turns and leaves and Sandy is left, standing once again in the middle of the room, waiting. Suddenly the door to the side of Lancaster opens and a man and woman step into the room.

Both are striking – she tall and slender, with very short, blond hair, practically a butch cut, and incredibly long, muscular, tanned legs that seem to have no end; he slightly shorter, heavily muscled, with the dark skin, fierce features and long, straight black hair of someone with significant Native American blood. A pair of black, leather, high heeled boots come to just below her sculpted calves, and the luscious thighs disappear into short, one-inch legs of a body hugging, one piece leotard. It is also black and made of what appears to be ribbed cotton, much like a man's undershirt, which the top of the garment looks like. Cut just above the nipples of her small breasts, it amply displays the sinewy muscles of her arms and shoulders, and is so tight and thin that the lips of her sex and pubic hair are visible through it. A similar suit stretches over his rippling physique, with the only difference being the legs reach to mid thigh. Sandy's eyes cannot leave the outline of the thick, heavy cock and balls pressing hard against the flimsy cloth.

"This is Elke and Jon. You, of course, will refer to them as Miss and Mr. They will work very closely with you while you are here, and will have the primary responsibility for your training. Others, such as myself, will be involved, but one or both of them will be with you much of the time. They are very good at what they do. You are very lucky to have been assigned to them. They are also demanding and uncompromising and you will do well to pay very close attention to everything they say and follow their directions, precisely and without hesitation."

Their flat, emotionless stares at her are unsettling, and after a few awkward moments she turns her head away.

"Please do not look away, Mrs. Howard. I want you to look directly at me." The woman's voice is heavily accented, but easily understandable, firm but soft.

Sandy stares back at her, fighting to hold her eyes steady. Lancaster's voice finally comes as a relief.

"Now, Mrs. Howard, we have the matter of what needs to be done to atone for the indifference, outright contempt and negligence you have recently displayed in your relationship with your husband - the reason you are here. Do you agree you have displayed these despicable traits, Mrs. Howard?"

"Not really. I mean, maybe a little, but this is mostly a game. Gregory says these things so he has a reason to, you know...play games, punish me. I came here mostly because they dared me. And they said it was going to be fun." She feels the resentment and anger come quickly to a boil. "I mean I'd get the hell out of here right now except there's no damned way I'm going to set myself up for Gregory to call me a wimp for the rest of his life."

"Miss Howard, you just can't remember much of anything, can you? How do you address everyone here?" His voice is suddenly shrill, loud; it startles her, and her anger turns to concern.

"Mr. Lancaster, I'm sorry sir. I should have said Mr. Lancaster."

"So you came on a dare. And they told you it was going to be fun?"

"Yes, Mr. Lancaster."

"Let me tell you a few things that are facts, Miss Howard. This is, in a way I suppose, a game, but we play it much more seriously than I suspect you ever have. And it can be fun, although that seems a rather shallow word for the level of intensity you will find here. You had better

136

prepare yourself to take this seriously. We do not suffer defiant, defensive, flippant, or uncooperative attitudes around here, and you will learn that very quickly. I was hoping you already had. I would bet you can be a very arrogant, haughty person when you want to be. Is that true, Mrs. Howard?"

She hesitates for a moment, her mind ricocheting between anger and good sense. "Yes, sometimes, Mr. Lancaster."

"You are free to leave, Mrs. Howard, but you must tell me now. This will be your last chance, one more than most have, but then I think you might be...as you say...more of a wimp than most. I suspect your husband is right about you, Mrs. Howard. What are you going to do, Mrs. Howard?"

Sandy feels the familiar, red-headed fire return in an instant. "I'm going to stay, Mr. Lancaster."

"Very well. Now, have you treated your husband in a manner that causes you to deserve to be punished?"

"Yes, Mr. Lancaster."

"Elke, would you please prepare Miss Howard for a thorough spanking with the strap." Lancaster rises from his chair and walks through the side door.

The woman moves forward, grabs Sandy's arm and leads her to the front of the desk. "Bend forward, please. Put your chest flat on the desk.

The leather top of the desk is cool against the bare skin of her stomach and cheek as she turns her head away from Jon's stare. Fingers slide under the waistband of the tap pants, and she feels the material being pulled down over her bottom, then down her legs.

"Step out of these, please." After they are off she feels a hand slip between her upper thighs. "Spread your legs slightly."

She waits, bent over the desk for what seems a long time, and then she hears the door open.

"Look up at me, Mrs. Howard."

She lifts her head and turns it to see Lancaster standing just behind the desk with a leather strap in his hand.

"Elke, secure her hands, please."

The woman comes around the desk and presses her hands against Sandy's, pinning then outstretched to the top of the desk. Lancaster takes the receiver off the phone, pushes a button, and speaks. "Gregory, are you there?"

"Yes, I am," comes the recognizable voice over the speaker.

"Gregory, your wife is about to be punished for the contemptible way she has treated you. Is there anything you would like to say to her or know from us?"

Sandy is mortified.

"Could you describe what you are going to do to her?"

"She is bent over the desk in my office. Her panties have just been removed and she is bare except for high heels and a very short blouse, which in this position exposes her breasts. Her legs are a bit apart, the cheeks of her bottom are stretched slightly open, and the lips of her sex are visible. Your wife is quite lovely, Gregory. Her hands are being held by Elke, one of her trainers. Jon, another trainer, will watch. I am going to give her a proper spanking with a leather strap."

"Have fun, darling. And don't wimp out and let me hear any sounds from you other than those of pleasure."

She wants to cry...from anger, and shame, and then she sees Lancaster step around to her side. Waiting, she presses her eyes tightly together.

"Open your eyes, Mrs. Howard, and look at me," Elke says.

She lifts her head, then feels the sharp sting as the strap lands on her bottom with a distinct 'crack'. There is a pause, then another sting, then another. He uses slow, measured strokes, but they are stronger that what she gets from Gregory, and after the first four or five she is tensing her buttocks and trying to squirm in anticipation of the next one. She wants to let out a gasp as another falls on the tender skin at the bottom of her cheeks, but she remembers Gregory, and then with the next slap of the strap she lets out a small cry anyway and jerks a foot from the floor.

Lancaster watches intently as Sandy's firm, round, creamy white buttocks flex and squeeze together in anticipation of the blows, then relax and squirm after each stroke of the strap, all the while reddening as the spanking continues. He now begins sliding the strap gently against the inside of her thighs, along the cleft between her cheeks, and against the red thatch and lips of her sex...between almost every stroke...and he looks for the telltale signs of arousal. It all seems to fall into a kind of rhythm, and after a few more blows he notices her movements are less frenetic and she is beginning to lift her ass ever so slightly to the strap. His arm pauses a little longer each time now, the spanking becomes more rhythmic, and not as hard. Her legs slide farther apart, there is a barely perceptible moan, and her glowing bottom arches even higher...to meet the caresses of the leather. The strap falls again and he watches as she moves her hips slowly from side to side, thrusting them up and back.

"Prepare Mrs. Howard for the first rehabilitation session please."

Elke releases her hands.

"Stand up, please," Jon says.

She does as she is told, the sting of the last couple of blows of the strap overwhelmed by the electric warmth flooding outward from her glistening pussy.

"Follow me, please." Jon leads the way through the door on the side of the office with Sandy behind him and Elke after her. They pass through what appears to be a small study, then into a room that has a high, flat, narrow table in the middle surrounded by three leather wing chairs. There are straps and restraints hanging from various spots on the ceiling and a large wardrobe against one wall.

"Lift your arms please," he says, and as she does Jon pulls her only remaining clothing, other than the high heels, over her head.

The table is covered with a white flannel sheet and Jon instructs her to get onto it and lie on her back. She follows his orders, and he then pulls a soft suede strap across her stomach and secures it to the other side of the table. The strap is snug but not tight, the table upholstered and comfortable. Elke grabs her ankles and lifts them up and Jon reaches for the side of the table and a section just beyond her buttocks folds down, effectively shortening the table and placing her ass at the very end. Elke lowers two black leather anklets attached to long, black leather thongs, attaches them and then Sandy feels her legs being pulled up until they are at perhaps a seventy five degree angle to her body, with her knees slightly bent. Her legs are then pulled slowly apart until there is about two feet between them – enough space for her to see Lancaster center one of the chairs just off the end of the table and sit down, her line of sight now framing his head between her upraised, parted thighs and above the perfect, triangular mound of red pubic hair.

"We're going to cover your eyes now, Mrs. Howard, and then start asking you some questions." Lancaster's voice is slower, more measured, gentler than she has heard it before. "It is very important that you relax completely and free your mind to be as honest with us as you can. We cannot help you attain your full sexual potential if you are not totally open and cooperative with us. This is the beginning of your instruction and training, and this first phase is crucially important. It can be a very pleasurable experience if you do exactly as you are told."

Sandy sees the blindfold as Elke lowers it and covers her eyes. It is comfortable, and like the strap across her stomach, snug but not tight. She is suddenly aware of soft, lilting, oriental music filling the room and the smell of incense. No one speaks for some time.

At first the touch is almost imperceptible, whatever is being brushed ever so lightly over her body. It starts at her neck, moves slowly down across her breasts, caresses, circles her nipples, then with a bit more pressure moves across her stomach, down the insides of her thighs, slowly back up, and along the lips of her sex.... now hesitating, now tickling, now probing. Possibly a feather, but whatever it is, Sandy feels the delicious tingle again....the heat.

Suddenly there is another sensation. A hot wetness slipping up along the lips of her pussy, licking, then sliding just inside. Hands are now on her breasts...large, firm hands, with fingers that caress her nipples. She feels a hardness press against her leg that she realizes is Jon's cock. The hot tongue sliding in and out of her is replaced by the head of John's cock...circling and probing her swollen clit...then slipping just inside the dripping lips...then back out...and back in. The mystery caress starts again. Slides down over her pussy, between the cheeks of her bottom. Sandy fights to slow her raging arousal.

Lancaster gazes at the glistening pink lips surrounded by the lovely thatch and pale, silky skin, nods at Elke, waits for her to move her gloved hand with the exotic feathers attached to the fingers back up to Sandy's breasts, and begins to speak. "Mrs. Howard, do you ever fantasize about sex?"

"Yes, Mr. Lancaster."

"How often?"

"Quite often, Mr. Lancaster."

"Do you fantasize about having sex with people other than your husband?"

"Sometimes, Mr. Lancaster."

"Do you fantasize about having sex with women?"

"Uh...no...not often, sir."

"Does it turn you on to think about women doing things

to your body, Mrs. Howard?"

"Uh, I don't think about that."

"Does it turn you on to think about another women's body?"

"I uh, don't think so,"

"Mrs. Howard, your answers are going to have to improve. You are not cooperating like you should. Please try to visualize what I am asking you and talk very freely about it."

The feathers play down her body again and now there is more pressure and probing as they again reach her sex. The glistening lips are pulled gently apart and the small bead is circled and tickled, again and again. The warm, electric sensation that she knows is a tongue is suddenly on her, licking gently at first but then harder, then penetrating and sucking…and she is ready to explode just as it stops. She lifts her hips to try and find it. After a few seconds the tongue probes her other lips; they quickly open and the heat and charge fills her mouth. Now the feathers start back across her breasts, then down between her legs, and to her glistening, swollen spot. The hot skin and weight of a body lowers onto her and as the two fiery tongues continue to embrace she feels another one begin to suck on her, hard. The crescendo builds again until once more, when she is within an instant of ecstasy and relief, everything stops. There is only the weight of the body.

"Mrs. Howard, would you like to cum?"

"Yes, Yes."

"Yes, what?"

"Yes, Mr. Lancaster."

The body slides up on her chest and she can feel the rough sensation of pubic hair.

"Now I want you to show me how much you want to cum by how well you use your mouth, Mrs. Howard, and by how hard you concentrate and how aroused you become. You've got to show me you're excited, Mrs. Howard. I'm not convinced yet that you are. Use your tongue, Mrs. Howard.

She puts her tongue out, feels it touch hair, skin, wetness...there is a salty, slightly tart taste, a perfumed, musky smell...then her mouth is covered with it.

"Your tongue, Mrs. Howard.

She begins to lick Elke's pussy, tentatively at first, then with more enthusiasm as her arousal spikes and she is again on the edge of orgasm.

"I'm afraid that's not hard enough, Mrs. Howard. Discipline her please."

Elke's warm, wet crotch suddenly lifts from her face, and the weight from her body, and Sandy feels her legs being lowered. The straps are loosened and she is turned over roughly, her feet dropping until they brush against the floor, her legs hanging down at a right angle to her body. Her ass is now draped across the edge of the table and there is little time before she feels the first blow of the paddle at the base of her buttocks. Again and again, in rapid succession, Jon slaps the flat wooden surface against her luscious, jutting cheeks. The sting causes her to gasp. The spanking is short, and when it is over she again feels a hand slide between her legs to her lips, then inside the folds, then another finger trace between her cheeks to her anus. The tiny opening is fondled for a few moments before Sandy feels the pressure and delicious sensation of her rectum being penetrated and filled. Two or three fingers move inside her vagina and ass in concert, probing and caressing her. This time she is sure she will cum before they can stop, but she is suddenly turned back over, her legs again raised with the straps, and Elke's sex covers her face once more.

"Now this time I want you to do a better job, Mrs. Howard."

Still highly aroused, she licks and sucks on the slick, dripping lips and clit as hard as she can, and when she turns her head for a moment to catch her breath she feels Elke again lift her weight from her. The blindfold is removed and she is staring directly, just inches away, at the matted blond hair and glistening pink petals, laid open, and the tiny engorged bulb, as Elke straddles her.

"Very well, Mrs. Howard. For someone who says she is not turned on by women, you are coming along quite nicely. Please turn around, Elke."

Sandy is still only inches from the woman's dripping sex, but now the trim, perfectly rounded buttocks are just in front of her eyes as Elke straddles her again, this time facing the end of the table.

"Now I want you to spread Elke's cheeks and work as hard with your tongue around her anus as you did on her vagina. If you do this well, Mrs. Howard, we might let you cum. It would be appropriate, I think. If you do not do well, you will be spanked again.

Sandy reaches up and pulls the lovely cheeks apart, revealing a tiny, pink, hairless, puckered opening. She has never been this close, and it startles her - how alluring, what a turn-on, the perfectly symmetrical, rounded curves of a woman's bottom and thighs, her pussy and anus, could be. Raising her head so her tongue can reach, she begins to circle, then lick Elke's behind. She hears a moan. She flicks her tongue again and again, then suddenly feels a mouth on her own sex, feels her spot being sucked, then something slide into her bottom. The delicious crescendo builds, continues to build, even when she is sure she has reached the top...keeps building...to a higher level of ecstasy than she has ever felt before. And then every inch of her body convulses. Again and Again.

"Mrs. Howard, you have exactly five minutes to get out of bed, brush your teeth, get your toiletries, and follow me." Miss Quinley is standing at the foot of the bed. Suddenly awakened by the woman's voice, Sandy is at first confused, unable for a few moments to recall where she is. Then it comes to her. Quinley hands her a short silk robe as Sandy throws her feet over the side of the bed. She hurriedly puts it on to hide her nakedness. After quickly brushing her teeth at the sink and splashing water on her face, she grabs the plastic bag, then follows Quinley's gesture and walks out of the room ahead of her.

"Go straight into the room at the end of the hall, Mrs. Howard."

As Sandy enters, Jon is standing by a wide table covered with a white plastic cover. He steps toward her, pulls the robe off her shoulders, and tells her to lie on the table on her stomach.

The table is wet with warm water. Only a moment after Sandy puts her head on her arm and turns it to the side, a flood of almost-hot, luxurious water washes over her. Then another. "This is our version of a bath, Mrs. Howard," Jon says, as he starts to soap her feet and legs with his hands. They move smoothly with the soap. His strong, yet caressing touch feels wonderful to Sandy as he moves up her thighs. Pushing her legs apart, both hands move up and down the inside of her thighs in unison. They move to her buttocks, kneading, scrubbing, slowly, then fingers slide down between her cheeks, and suddenly her anus is penetrated as she feels a soapy, slippery finger inside her. Jon's cleansing is thorough, but gentle. Wonderful. Another spray of water splashes over her. *Nothing wrong with this. Nothing at all. Oh yeah! This is what the hell Gregory needs to see.* Jon continues and washes her back and neck, but spends less time there than on her bottom.

"Turn over, Mrs. Howard."

After Sandy has followed Jon's orders, her eyes lock on the huge bulge of his cock and balls behind the flimsy material covering them. It's the same one piece, thin cotton outfit as he wore yesterday. Today it's white. Sandy glances up at the hard, well-defined chest, flat stomach, the muscular thighs flowing from the shorts that end a couple of inches down his legs. But her gaze quickly returns to his stunning crotch. She can easily see the outline of Jon's swollen cock with its bulging head, held down and to the side by the material as it strains to escape. And the inflated sack holding his balls. A bucket of warm water floods across her body and face, causing her to cough as some enters her nose and mouth.

Jon washes her hair, expertly massaging and kneading

her scalp with his strong hands. Soapy fingers slide smoothly over her breasts and nipples, then linger. Her stomach is next, and soon his fingers are probing the red triangle of wet, matted hair. "Spread you legs, Mrs. Howard."

Slowly, Sandy slides her feet apart and spreads her thighs. It is all she can do to keep from climaxing as his fingers slide along the lips of her pussy and the luxurious cleansing continues inside her. Jon neglects nothing, and his fingers brush again and again over her clit as he works down and up her thighs, to the thatch of hair, then the folds, and inside her. Just enough to tease. Sandy turns her head to the side, lets out a soft moan, and is suddenly only inches from Jon's cock, still straining mightily to escape the shorts. There is a noticeable wet spot on the material. She longs to touch it...pull it out...take it into her mouth... see it in all its glory...pull it into her. God, she wants to explode.

"Enough, Jon." The familiar voice of Lancaster startles Sandy. "We've a lot planned for Mrs. Howard today."

Sandy feels woozy from her abruptly terminated, unfulfilled state of arousal as she re-enters the hall, her robe back on.

"Please, please stop." The voice is one of pleading, but compromised by heavy breathing, and Sandy sees it is coming from a tiny figure just ahead of her. The girl is small and slender. She has long, jet black hair that is hanging to the floor as she is draped across the lap of a muscular, swarthy, bearded man, dressed like Jon. The trainer is seated in a chair in the hall.

The man's hand descends again and again - in rapid fire

succession. The girl is being spanked soundly, as her squirms indicate. "Go into you room, Mrs. Howard", Lancaster says, as Sandy slows her steps. As they pass, Sandy casts one last look at the reddened bottom. Being so slender, arched across the trainer's lap, her ass cheeks are parted and the small, puckered opening has the same dark hue as her friend Donna's bottom when she is bent over for a spanking. The thought flashes through Sandy's mind that this is indeed a far different take on the games that the two couples have played.

Once inside Sandy's room, Lancaster closes the door behind them, then tells Sandy to sit in the straight-baked chair against the wall.

"Very well, Mrs. Howard, did you enjoy your bath?"

"Yes, Mr. Lancaster."

"Did you cum while Jon was washing you, Mrs. Howard?"

"No, Mr. Lancaster."

"Very good. I do believe you might be learning. Now, part of your husband's complaint is that you have not been very sexually attentive to him. He says you are not imaginative enough, don't try to turn him on that often, and when you do, you do not take care of him sexually as well as you should. Not nearly as well as he takes care of you. Do you think he is right, Mrs. Howard?"

The anger comes quickly, but so does restraint. And a calmness. "I don't agree with that, Mr. Lancaster."

"Do you like to turn your husband on, Mrs. Howard."

"Yes, Mr. Lancaster."

"It is the duty of a wife, or husband, or lover, to be diligent in working to turn their partner on, Mrs. Howard. Of course, if done successfully, both partners benefit. But you should always be conscious of the need to make him want you, Mrs. Howard. You may need to do it every day, or every other day, or once a week. It depends on how often he needs it. And it doesn't matter how much he loves you or how much you love him. You still have to work on it, create an environment of eroticism. Most men, and more women than you might think, due to the Creator's hard wiring and cultural influences, require varied methods of stimulation. You must always realize every partner has to make it their job to provide this stimulation, because it's a necessary component of enjoying the sexual pleasure both partners want. It's your duty. Just as it's his duty to do the same. Do you understand?"

"Yes, Mr. Lancaster."

"You may turn him on by what you wear, by what you say, by touching him. By what you do, the way you act. It does not matter, as long as you always remember it is your duty to turn him on."

"Now, having established your obligation to turn your partner on - during our training session this morning we are going to skip past the various ways you might do that, and concentrate on what you do after you have turned him on. We are going to concentrate on what you do when it's your turn to give him pleasure. We are going to assume you have a partner who, when you treat him well, will be extraordinarily good at giving you a great deal of sexual pleasure, and on many occasions. We are now going to deal with what you will do to pleasure him when it's your turn. When you want it to be your turn. Or if he has decided it will be your turn. Another reason we are going to leave the session on turning your partner on until later is that I believe Jon may already be well along that path this morning. Do you concur, Mrs. Howard?"

Sandy starts to look over at Jon, then thinks better of it. "Yes, Mr. Lancaster.

"Very well. I am not going to waste time by seeing how you would normally give pleasure, Mrs. Howard. I'm going to take Gregory at his word that you do not put much effort into it. We will tell you what to do."

Elke enters the room, stands with her back against the wall facing Sandy, and says nothing.

"Stand up, Mrs. Howard. Jon..."

Jon steps directly in front of Sandy.

"Remove her clothing."

Jon slowly removes the robe, then his hands gently touch her breasts and his finger tips begin circling her nipples. He leans over and his tongue flicks against the smooth skin, then circles. Sandy feels the heat return. Jon drops to his knees. His tongue starts up her left leg, his fingers up her right. Over her calves, knees, thighs. His hand suddenly pushes up, she spreads her legs slightly, and his fingers touch, then slide up and down her wet lips. Jon stands and puts his lips to Sandy's. They share a long, hot kiss as his fingers continue to explore and caress her pussy. Then Jon pulls back.

"Caress his neck and shoulders, Mrs. Howard. Lightly." Sandy is aware of her sexual temperature rising as she caresses the massive muscles under Jon's taut, smooth skin. "Now run your fingers across his breasts and nipples. Again, lightly. Try to feel as much of them as you can through the material. Concentrate on making your touch penetrate the material."

Sandy does as she is told.

"The idea is to start lightly. And a bit away from the most sensitive area, the area that he can't wait until you touch. Or lick. Then move closer, still with a light touch. Then become firmer with your touch and caresses. . Now pull his top down just below his abdomen."

Sandy pulls the sleeveless material down to reveal his smooth, muscular chest, and erect nipples. She continues down over the rock hard stomach and stops the material just below his belly button. She doesn't have to be told to continue caressing his beautiful body. Her hands continue as she leans forward and begins with her tongue. She plays with his nipples, the sparse hair on his chest. She leaves enough saliva in his belly button to make it glisten.

"Now his crotch, Mrs. Howard. And remember, slowly."

Sandy hooks her fingers inside the material.

"No, Mrs. Howard. Through the material at first."

Sandy feels the thin patch of pubic hair as she slowly slides her hand over the single layer of cotton, and the question of whether he shaves flashes through her mind. She very gently cups the swollen cock and balls, thrills to the feel of their bulk and hardness, then pulls her hands back and begins lightly tracing their outline with her fingers, then circling, then brushing."

"Excellent. Now you can be a bit more firm, Mrs. Howard"

Jon moans softly. Sandy is mesmerized as she caresses him.

"Now I want you to suck him through the material, Mrs. Howard. Remember, lightly at first. Then harder."

Sandy drops to her knees. She aches to devour Jon. It's only the "lightly at first" that could be a problem. But she follows directions and is rewarded with more groans and movement from Jon. She licks at first, then flicks her tongue, then licks again. Suddenly she has as much of the material and his cock in her mouth as she can manage. She starts to suck.

"Pull his cock out, Mrs. Howard."

Sandy pulls her face back. She slides her hand up the leg of his shorts and slowly encircles his cock with her fingers. It feels magnificent. She pulls it out as she pushes the leg of the shorts up over his balls. Sandy can't remember a more beautiful sight. Jon's cock is thick, upturned at a slight angle, and pulsing. It looks huge, alive. The head is large, reddish, beautiful. A drop of glistening seamen hangs on the tip. The sack holding his balls is full. Sandy stares for a moment, then slowly encircles his balls with her hand and lowers her mouth over his throbbing cock. She takes it deep into her mouth, and begins sucking. Gently at first, as Lancaster instructed her.

"Mrs. Howard, you need to lick him first. Then suck on him. Do you understand? You are going too fast."

Sandy pulls her mouth off.

"I want you to only lick him now. Do you understand, Mrs. Howard?"

"Yes, Mr. Lancaster."

It's all Sandy can do not to fully engulf Jon again. But she only licks, and nibbles, and caresses with her fingers.

"Now, tell Jon to turn around."

"Please turn around, Jon", Sandy says.

"Now I want you to start at his neck and work your way down. Then after a few moments of that, start at his calves with your fingers and tongue and move up his legs. And remember, slowly."

Sandy is impatient, but follows Lancaster's orders. As quickly as she thinks will be tolerated, she has her hands under the legs of his shorts and is touching the bottom of the cheeks of his ass. Lancaster says nothing and she begins to rub her hands over the firm rounded buttocks under the white material. Her thumb slides between his cheeks and she presses down until she can feel the sparse thatch that she knows surrounds his anus.

"Strip him, Mrs. Howard."

Thank you. At last

Sandy quickly pulls the one-piece tights down until Jon raises his feet to step out of it. She doesn't need any instruction here. After kneading his buttocks a few quick times, she starts licking her tongue up and down along each cheek, next to his crack. Slowly her tongue moves closer, then she lets it slide down between his cheeks. She pulls her head back, then slowly spreads the firm buttocks until she can clearly see the small, puckered opening. Sliding her hand between his legs, she gently wraps her fingers around his rock-hard cock and swollen balls.

"Mrs. Howard, tell Jon to get up on the bed on his hands and knees."

"Yes, Mr. Lancaster."

"Jon, please get up on the bed on your hands and knees."

Jon does as he is told. Sandy is transfixed for a moment by the sight of his arched ass, his legs spread enough so that his beautiful cock and balls hang heavy and visible between them.

"You are doing quite well, Mrs. Howard. Perhaps your husband was a little off the mark. Now I want you to start caressing his cock, his balls, and his ass at the same time, Mrs. Howard."

Sandy steps to the side of the bed, her eyes locked on the vulnerability of Jon's arched ass and the steel of his manhood. She envelops his cock and balls with one hand, then runs a finger over his anus, then circles it. John's moans are louder now.

"Now keep caressing his cock and balls, and tell him to spread his cheeks."

"Yes, Mr. Lancaster.

"Spread you cheeks, Jon."

Jon reaches back, spreads his bottom wide open, and now Sandy is staring at his anus.

"I want you to lubricate him, then push your finger into him as far as you can, Mrs. Howard."

Sandy looks around for lubricant.

"You're not following my instructions, Mrs. Howard."

"I'm sorry."

"You're what?"

"I'm sorry, Mr. Lancaster."

"I won't tolerate those mistakes. Not on your second day. Now, lubricate your finger and put it up into him."

Sandy looks again for lubricant.

"Now! Mrs. Howard. You can never go more than a moment without touching him."

Sandy reaches down and drenches her finger in the folds of her dripping pussy, pulls it out and places it against Jon's anus, then pushes it slowly, but deeply, into him. He's tight. He suddenly squeezes the muscles of his sphincter against her finger, and the sensation causes her to moan with pleasure.

"Keep caressing his cock and balls, Mrs. Howard. And again, start slowly in his rectum. In and out. Then harder."

Sandy no longer hears Lancaster. She feels herself ready to explode, pulls her hand away from Jon's cock and reaches for her clit.

"Elke!" Lancaster's voice is sharp.

Suddenly Sandy is pulled away from Jon. Her finger slides out of his tight, slick bottom. She is quickly pulled across Elke's lap and the first sharp slap across her bottom makes her gasp. Instinctively, she squirms and tries to shift her bottom to escape the blows.

"Hold still, Mrs. Howard. You are not being spanked as hard as you should be. Although you will be if you don't obey me. When you are being punished, you will hold perfectly still if I tell you to. And I am telling you to. Do you understand?"

"Yes, Mr. Lancaster." Sandy's voice sounds weak.

"Mrs. Howard, you would like to cum, wouldn't you?"

Elke suddenly stops the spanking.

"Yes, Mr. Lancaster."

"Would you like Jon's cock to fill you up?"

"Oh yes, Mr. Lancaster."

"Overall, you've done very well, Mrs. Howard. Only a few minor mistakes. And you've been punished for those. Now perhaps we will show you we can also reward good behavior. Jon. Elke."

Elke leaves Sandy bent across her lap, and pushes her legs apart. Sandy sees Jon in front of her now, his hard cock at an angle as it is too heavy to stand straight out. He has a slender, four inch vibrator in his hand and a jar of Vaseline. He looks Sandy in the eye and begins to lubricate the vibrator. He steps around behind her. Sandy feels her cheeks being spread, then the vibrator against her anus, then the sensation of it being pushed into her rectum. The feeling of being filled completely, tightly, is delicious. It begins to vibrate; she hears the low hum.

Lancaster's cock pushes against his pants as he looks at the sight before him. Sandy's milky white, full, round cheeks are arched, spread, and the vibrator is in her bottom. The pink lips of her pussy glisten - the lips themselves slightly parted and swollen with her excitement, and surrounded by the lovely thatch of hair.

"Stand up, bend forward, and lean your hands against the wall, Mrs. Howard."

Sandy does as she is told. Elke holds the vibrator in

place in her bottom as she stands and gets into the new position. She feels Jon's hands spread her legs wider apart...then his tongue along the lips of her dripping pussy...and flick across her clit. Her arousal spikes in intensity. Suddenly his thick, steel-hard dick slides into her pussy from behind, then pushes deep inside her. The feeling of her bottom and pussy both filled...the movements, the vibration...is too much. With the eighth or ninth thrust, Sandy explodes.

The cool freshness of the silk comforter feels good against her skin as she lies, naked, face down on the bed in her room. The leftover sensations from the spanking Elke gave her, the vibrator, and her explosive climax are still noticeable. Elke's touch is very pleasant and soothing as she gently rubs a wonderfully scented lotion into Sandy's buttocks. "To ease the sting, dear."

Soft strains of a Celtic flute fill the room, and Sandy's mind drifts to the implications of her current weekend adventure. She will surely be a lot better at pleasuring Gregory. She imagines his startled look and then his groans of pleasure as she slips the vibrator up into his ass, then pulls his dick deep into her mouth, all the while playing with his balls. He'll be pleased, but he'll also learn very quickly that she's going to expect a lot more from him. He's going to have to learn to be as good as Jon and Elke together, or he might have to find someone else to help him pleasure her. She's never been as turned on, as crazy with lust, or had the kind of cataclysmic orgasm she had just an hour ago. Now that she's had a taste of it...

"I'm not supposed to say anything, but can you keep a secret? Elke's voice is as soft as a little girl's whisper.

"Sure," Sandy replies, almost in a purr.

"I really like you. I love your body, and your skin. It's so smooth. I love touching you. And I really liked it when you licked me yesterday. I'm sorry if the spankings I give you hurt, but I get in big trouble if Lancaster thinks I'm too lenient."

"Don't worry. It's beginning to turn me on more than it hurts. And I know you have to." Sandy instinctively reaches her hand back and touches Elke's thigh. "Does Lancaster punish you if you disobey him?"

"You've got that right. Most of the guests who come here - I don't mind punishing them. The men, and some of the women - I usually get into it. But you're different. You look so...vulnerable. And you get tears in your eyes so easily."

"So how did you end up here?" Sandy asks.

"I was doing some modeling for a fetish magazine, and one thing led to another."

"For the money, or because you're into it?"

"Both, I guess. My best friend in high school, we were in our mid teens, and she had this incredibly hot step father. He was a right wing religious type, a lay preacher...had been a professional rugby player...looked like Sean Connery. Also a real "Great Santini" type. Believed his duty to the family was to be sure Susan and her brothers got plenty of discipline. She never told me it turned her on, but she seemed to delight in relating the details. She usually knew ahead of time, had to wait until he got home. He would take his belt off, that was the sign, then take her to her room. He would make her take her pants or skirt off, then he would pull down her panties. She had to lay across his lap. I'd lay awake at night masturbating, fantasizing about him spanking me."

Elke continued. "In my early twenties I was with a guy for a few years who was really into it. Understood all the rituals, the role playing. We had an incredible sexual relationship, with a lot of erotic discipline. But he was crazy, neurotic, did a lot of drugs and alcohol. Wouldn't quit. I had to leave."

"But you're giving out most of the discipline here," Sandy says.

"Well, I learned once I got here that I can like it both ways. It's just a mindset, and I've always been very open minded about receiving and giving pleasure. And besides, the money's pretty good."

"So it's all a turn on, all fun," asks Sandy.

"Oh no. Most of our guests don't look like you. It can be work. But if I open my mind enough I can find some pleasure with most anyone, or at least satisfaction in a job well done. Then there are Lancaster's punishments for the staff. They can border on harsh, but I guess I do usually get aroused at some point."

"Tell me about who else is here now."

"Well," Elke hesitates for a moment, "there are two other ladies, and one man. Jennifer, she was a real bitch right from the start. Kept saying she thought we were all perverts, that the only reason she was here was her boyfriend had bet her $5,000 she couldn't take it. Admitted she's been spoiled rotten all her life."

"So how's she doing?," Sandy whispers.

"She got very upset during her examination and refused to cooperate. Quinley wasn't available, so Lancaster called me in. He of course gave her the option to leave, and when she refused, he told her he would do whatever was necessary to complete the examination. Lancaster and I held her down while Rawls did his thing. She began to relax and get a little turned on when Rawls fingers were in her pussy, but when we bent her over the end of the table and Rawls told her to spread her cheeks for her rectal exam, she started yelling and fighting again. Lancaster told us to hold her, and then he took his belt off and gave her as thorough a spanking as I've ever seen him give anyone that's just arrived."

"What happened then?"

"She bawled like a baby. Lancaster's amazing. After spanking her until her ass was red, he spoke to her very calmly, and within a few minutes she was apologizing and bending over the table without having to be held down. When Rawls put the glove on, lubricated his finger and told her to spread her cheeks - she didn't hesitate for a second. Anyway, I really looked forward to spanking her."

"Elke!" The voice startled Sandy.

"Oh, uh...yes, sir", Elke's reply was weak, frightened.

"This is the second issue this week. You know the rules. Be in the back room at three o'clock sharp." The door they had never heard open now shut sharply behind Lancaster.

"Jesus." Elke mutters under her breath.

"What's going to happen?"

"I can't say anything else, but you'll find out. That's

161

for sure." Elke starts rubbing the lotion onto Sandy again. During her description of Jennifer's examination, and likely while Lancaster was watching, her fingers had slipped into the crevasse between Sandy's cheeks, then down to the lips of her pussy, and lingered, with soft caresses. Now they are all business, rubbing across her hips. After a few more minutes, Elke quickly leaves without a word

It is 12:00 noon when Rawls walks unannounced into Sandy's room and startles her from a brief nap. "Follow me, Mrs. Howard."

She stumbles to her feet. "Can I at least brush my teeth? I've been asleep."

"Certainly. But no more than a few minutes."

Sandy enters the hallway and Rawls is waiting for her. He turns, walks a few steps, then through the door to the right. She finds herself once again in the examination room.

"Because of your behavior yesterday, we had to skip a procedure during your entrance physical. I'll take care of that now. You've noticed that the meals here are very healthy. We want to ensure that your body is as healthy and clean as your new perspective on sexuality." Rawls pulls the tall stand with the red bag and tube to the end of the examination table.

"What are you going to do?" Sandy asks, alarm in her voice.

"I'm going to give you an enema, Mrs. Howard."

"No, goddamit." Sandy is suddenly flushed with knee-jerk anger, turns and stalks back through the door. Then it

162

hits her. What has she done? What will happen? It's Rawls, who turned her on with his examination only yesterday. She freezes for a moment in the hall, conflicting feelings flooding her mind. She steps back into the examination room.

"I'm sorr…sorry."

Rawls face shows no expression. "You realize what that kind of outburst means, don't you Mrs. Howard?"

"You don't have to tell Mr. Lancaster, do you?"

"We'll see about that. Now step out of your shoes, take your panties off and lie on your left side on the table with your legs slightly bent."

Sandy does as she is told, and as she settles down onto the cool sheet, she is aware that the door to the room is still open. He bare bottom and legs are exposed to the open door, and Rawls moves the stand with the bag to the side of the table, then moves directly in front of her and slowly, methodically, pulls on a rubber glove. He is just as methodical as he lubricates his gloved finger, then he steps around behind Sandy.

Rawls eyes are locked on the tiny waist rising dramatically to the perfectly curved hip, then down again to the shapely, muscular thighs. The skin of her bottom is velvety smooth, milky white and unblemished, and in this position there is only a slight glimpse of the red thatch peeking from below her cheeks. Placing his left hand on her behind, he uses his fingers to spread her cheeks slowly, until they are wide open and the tiny opening is available and waiting.

Sandy feels the cool air on her anus with her cheeks

spread, and the anticipation of what will come next causes a faint stirring of arousal. She feels the slick gloved finger touch her, press gently, then slide up into her bottom. The lips of her sex also feel a light brushing sensation. Rawls finger slides back out and she feels what she knows is the tube slowly replace it. The light caresses of her now wet pussy continue, and Sandy suddenly gives in to the fact that she is being given the first enema of her adult life, with her naked bottom, protruding tube and bag visible to anyone who might walk by – and she is turned on. The warm water begins to enter her, and she discovers yet another sensation of pleasure and another elevation of arousal.

Rawls is very business like during the enema, with the exception of continuing to lightly caress the slick pink lips exposed just below the white tube. Almost as if this was a necessary part of any enema. He makes no additional move toward arousing Sandy further, and as soon as he removes the tube he tells her she can be excused.

She is still aroused when she returns to find him sitting on the chair against the wall. "You may put your panties and shoes back on now, Mrs. Howard, and return to your room. I will be in within a few minutes to deal with that unfortunate outburst before you got control of yourself."

Sandy sits on the bed in her room, no more than ten minutes after leaving the examination room, and her thoughts about what just happened, Rawls, and what may be about to happen, cause her hand to slip under the wide leg of the tap pants and find her tiny bud of pleasure. While contemplating for a moment whether she dare allow herself to cum, Rawls is suddenly in front of her.

"Well now, that must not have been such a bad

experience after all," he says with a wry smile.

She quickly pulls her hand from inside her panties.

"I'm going to grant you a reprieve. I won't tell Lancaster about your behavior. But I will give you a very thorough paddling myself." Rawls closes the door behind him and pulls the wooden, straight back chair from against the wall. As he sits down he motions for Sandy to rise, then tells her to get across his lap. As she bends forward, he positions her so that her bottom is jutting up and her pubic mound is between his slightly parted legs. "You deserve a sound spanking Mrs. Howard, and you're going to get one."

Sandy feels his fingers slide under the waistband of her panties before he pulls them down to just below her knees. Rawls gently places his hand across her buttocks and one of his fingers slips down to rest on the lips of her pussy, now dripping again. "Were you spanked as a child or teenager, Mrs. Howard?"

"No."

"So your first experience, or most of your spankings, have come from your husband?"

"Yes. But he doesn't spank me as hard as the spankings here."

"Well, maybe he should spank you as hard, or as often. If you're honest, it hasn't been all bad - what's happened to you here, has it?"

"Well, no, I mean…I guess not."

"You guess not? You're about to get a thorough spanking and you're dripping wet. Don't lie to me, Mrs.

Howard. It will make things worse."

"Yes…it hasn't been all bad."

The spanking is hard, but not unpleasant. In between each three or four blows, Rawls fingers find their way back between Sandy's legs, gently sliding across her clit. Rawls spreads his legs slightly and she can feel his rock hard cock pressing against her pubic mound. Sandy starts to lift her bottom to the blows and abandons any attempt to stifle her moans.

Rawls eyes lock on the stunning sight of Sandy's ass, only inches away, rising and falling, her reddening cheeks parting enough to reveal glimpses of the tiny bud of her anus. The pink lips of her pussy glisten with her excitement.

"Stand up and bend over the bed, Mrs. Howard. I'm going to take off my belt."

Sandy scrambles off his lap and bends over, placing her hands on the edge of the bed. She can hear him unbuckle his belt and slide it off.

"No. What I'm going to do, what I want to do, is fuck you. I'm not supposed to, but I want to fuck you more than anyone who has ever been here."

She feels his dick slide up over her cheeks, then along her crack. As hot and horny as she can remember, she blurts, "Jeffrey told me I was going to have fun, so damn him. Fuck me! Fuck me hard!!" Within an instant she feels Rawls fill her pussy, push deeper, then begin to slide in and out with powerful strokes. The pleasure is exquisite, divine. She wants to scream.

The knock on Sandy's door is precisely at 2:55 p.m.

Miss Quinley leads her down the hall to the room at the back of the building. There are two other women already inside, both dressed in the same short white top, panties and heels. Sandy wonders which is Jennifer. The tiny, slender cutie, with jet black hair to her shoulders and large, doe like eyes, probably in her late twenties, the same lady who was getting a spanking in the hall...or the somewhat older blond, with striking, sharp, movie-star quality facial features, a full hipped, voluptuous figure, and perfectly tapered legs. The blonde's gorgeous face, tilted slightly up in what might be considered a hint of arrogance, is Sandy's only clue.

There is also a man with a rather plain but attractive face, balding, and a bodybuilder's physique. He has on a pair of small, thin, white bikini underpants and his dick, balls and pubic hair are clearly visible through the filmy material. Suddenly Jon and another male and female trainer come into the room. Everyone stands against the wall, the trainers on one side, Sandy and the others across from them. There is a table in the middle of the room, padded and covered with a white sheet, the same as the table where Sandy had her first "instructional session."

Rawls comes into the room, dressed in his lab coat, pushing the metal rack on wheels with the red bag and white tube. Sandy feels her body tense and a warm tingling between her legs. Is it the beautiful Rawls, the apparatus with the bag that she has experienced, the others in the room, or the apprehension over what is going to happen next?

Elke walks into the room with her head down, in her trainer's leotard and short, heeled boots, goes to the far corner, and stands with her back to the others. Lancaster

167

arrives within seconds, and announces solemnly that Elke has broken rules with the guests twice within the past week. He makes it clear that trainers are subject to their own rules, and violations of these rules are dealt with firmly.

"Elke, come here."

Elke turns and moves to the center of the room. Her eyes now lift to meet Lancaster's.

"Take off your leotard, please. Leave the boots on."

Elke pulls the leotard down over her beautiful breasts, the nipples hard and erect, then over her hips, down her thighs, and steps out of them. Her body is stunning, the golden triangle of pubic hair the perfect decoration at the top of her long, muscular legs and below the flat, silky skin of her stomach. She holds her hands by her side, and stands very erect.

For a moment Sandy can't shift her eyes from the glorious female flesh in front of her. Then she quickly glances around. The cocks of the two trainers are clearly hard, but the man to Sandy's right is so erect that the waistband of his briefs has pulled away from his abdomen and pubic hair is visible above it. Sandy presses her thighs closer together to hide the slippery wetness.

"On the table, Elke, on your stomach, please."

All eyes are on the gorgeous body as she turns and places one leg up on the table. She is up on her stomach quickly, but not before her movement offers a fetching glimpse of the pink lips of her vagina and the tiny, puckered opening as her buttocks spread.

"To our guests, please don't assume the punishment

Elke is about to receive is reserved only for trainers who have misbehaved. That would be a mistake. She is going to be spanked very soundly, but first we are going to give her something to think about. We want to be sure she is very focused while she is being punished. That way she is less likely to repeat her misbehavior. Mr. Rawls."

Rawls steps forward and begins to pull a rubber glove from his pocket onto his right hand. Out of the other pocket he produces a tube of KY lubricant. After unscrewing the cap, he lubricates his gloved index finger, holding the digit up, moving slowly and deliberately. After everyone has ample time to let the significance of what is about to happen sink in, Rawls speaks in a steady, level tone. "Please spread your cheeks, Elke."

She reaches back, puts one hand on each of her trim, muscular, white buttocks, and pulls them apart. Sandy is aware of the man on her right inching closer to a position behind Elke. A quick glance shows her his huge cock is close to escaping above the waistband of his briefs. Sandy's eyes return to Elke in time to see Rawls push his finger up into her rectum. She is completely still, holding her cheeks spread apart, for the moments he leaves his finger inside her - longer than necessary to adequately lubricate her.

When Rawls does remove his finger, he tells her to get on her hands and knees. She obeys. There is now a new, incredibly alluring pose exposing the full glory of her pubic hair and glistening pink lips below her exquisitely rounded, arched bottom. Rawls pulls the metal frame with the bag to his side, uncoils the white plastic tube, and covers the slender nozzle with lubricant.

"Miss Howard, will you please help Mr. Rawls by holding Elke's cheeks apart so he can insert the nozzle."

Sandy is momentarily startled at the mention of her name. But she recovers and acts quickly, stepping across to stand by Rawls. He nods to her, and she gingerly puts her hands on Elke's cheeks, then slowly pulls them apart. At the very moment that the lovely little opening is fully revealed, Sandy realizes she might cum. She swallows hard. Rawls places the tip of the nozzle on the puckered bud and pushes slowly. It disappears into Elke's behind until the rim is all that is visible. Sandy again takes a deep breath and steps back.

Rawls stands motionless for a moment, again as if to let the scene sink in, then reaches up and unsnaps the clamp that releases the water. As the bag empties, Elke begins to moan slightly. Rawls, at about the point the bag is half emptied, clamps it off, then reaches between her legs, brushing across her pussy, and massages her lower abdomen. After a few moments, he unclamps the bag again, and once again Elke moans. Sandy doesn't know where she is supposed to be, or what she is supposed to do, but she is transfixed by the sight of the tube jutting from Elke's bottom, and her moans, so she stays still. When the bag is empty, Rawls stands back for a moment, then slowly slides the nozzle from Elke's behind. Sandy now stares at the puckered opening, glistening with lubricant, and shudders as her orgasm grips her too quickly to stop.

"Now, Elke, everyone is going to get to see what kind of control you have." Lancaster's voice was light, almost mocking in tone. "Stand down and bend over the end of the table."

Sandy steps further back as Elke slides off of the table, straining to keep her legs pressed together. She sees the leather strap in Lancaster's hand, and for the first time realizes that Elke is going to be spanked while filled with the enema. Even before the first slap of the strap across her bottom, the concentration of Elke trying to keep her legs together is clear to all in the room. She raises her chest up, then back down against the table, sinking down and then back up with her knees. The gorgeous blond woman squirms as Lancaster keeps applying the strap to her rapidly reddening bottom.

Finally, mercifully, Lancaster puts the strap down on the table. "You may go to the restroom, my dear."

Elke is through the door in a flash.

"Miss Howard", Lancaster suddenly turns to Sandy, who has moved back against the wall, "Elke misbehaved by talking to you this morning. Did she tell you that she was breaking the rules?"

Sandy is stunned. She feels every eye in the room on her. "I...I don't..."

"Speak up, Miss Howard. It's a simple question. Did Elke tell you she was not supposed to talk to you?"

"Yes sir, she did."

"Then you should not have let her continue. You should have told her you were not going to be a part of a violation of a rule."

"But, Mr. Lancaster...I"

"Do you agree, Miss Howard? You should not have been a willing party to a violation of a rule that you had just been told was being broken."

"Yes, Mr. Lancaster."

"And you just climaxed without being told to, isn't that true, Mrs. Howard?"

"Ye...yes, Mr. Lancaster."

"Step out here, Miss Howard."

Sandy, visibly shaking, does as she is told.

"Take your clothes off, Miss Howard."

Sandy doesn't move for a moment, and in that moment contradictory thoughts race through her mind. *Only one more full day and I'll be back at home and away from this craziness. But if I let myself relax, what's going to happen next is going to make me explode again, with a new level of ecstasy. Crazy...but I've never had such pleasure.*

"Now, Miss Howard." Lancaster's voice sharpens noticeably as Sandy hesitates. She quickly pulls off her top, then pushes her panties down and steps out of them.

"Jon, Robert." Lancaster motions for the two trainers to move to the center of the room. "Before I punish Mrs. Howard, I want the two of you to ravish her body with your hands, tongues, maybe even those beautiful cocks that I notice are rather revealing of your state of arousal. I want to see how high you can take Mrs. Howard, how well she can then follow directions regarding controlling her orgasm. If she does well she may only get a spanking. If not, she could suffer Elke's fate. At some point I would like to see her mouth, pussy and ass filled at the same time.

As she stands in front of Lancaster and the others in the room, completely naked, with her hands to her side, she feels a tear begin to well up...but also increasing heat in her loins. She realizes for the first time the connection. Not a tear of fear, or anger, but a tear of emotion as she once again feels the intense, anxiety driven sexual run-up that was unknown to her until the last two days.

Jon starts by sliding his tongue down the small of her back, traces the crevice between her cheeks, then moves lower to the inside of her thigh, as he kneels. Robert is licking and flicking his tongue across her nipples as his hand slides between her legs and his fingers gently probe the wet folds for her clit. Tilting her head back, she moans. Over the next ten, fifteen, twenty minutes – Sandy loses all track of time – she feels fingers and tongues slide in and out of her pussy, caresses cover her breasts and nipples, deep, hot, probing kisses, and her bottom gently penetrated, often simultaneously.

She ends up on the table on her hands and knees, with Jon below her, licking her folds, sucking her clit while he massages her breasts, and Robert in back of her, gently probing her ass with a finger. When she has successfully fought off climaxing more than once amidst the luxurious fog of sexual heat that floods her body, she lets her mind wander. She knows she is going to be spanked in front of these people. Doesn't mind. Welcomes it. She knows the pleasure will come again in waves. And then, at some point, the exquisite orgasm...or orgasms.

She wonders if it will ever be the same when she is home with Gregory. Will sex be boring compared to this? Will she need this? Giving up control. The intensity. The wantonness.

Standing directly in back of the table, Lancaster's eyes

are glued to Sandy as she lies very still. Her lush, round, jutting buttocks are still slightly parted from the invasion of Robert's finger, and he glimpses the tiny pink bud, the open, beckoning glove of her sex, and knows what he must do, what everyone expects...knows that he must punish her.

Lancaster reaches for the leather strap and says, in as stern a voice as he can muster, "Mrs. Howard, please get off the table and bend over the end of it."

Watching as Sandy follows his orders, he realizes he has rarely, if ever, seen as lovely a lady...so gorgeous...such an amazing body...such raw sexuality. And he can't remember ever wanting so desperately to strip off his clothes and make love to someone. Spanking her again will only incense his raging desire. The discipline, the examinations...with Sandy it has been a new level of arousal for him. But who is really in charge here? Lancaster knows she is the one having epic, exquisitely sublime sexual adventures that will likely change her life forever...that will give her opportunities for levels of erotic ecstasy and fulfillment she wasn't aware existed. But, alas, that will also put her squarely in the sights of sexual scrutiny and self-doubt.

A year after the events in the story you have just read took place, Sandy started writing erotica, and was immediately successful. She stayed in touch with Lancaster and he agreed to contribute to the present tense narrative of that weekend that opened her eyes so wide to the possibilities of exquisite pleasure through erotic discipline...and so changed her life.

Through incessant challenges and harassment, she was

also able to convince Jeffrey to spend a weekend at the Center, and later to work there with her one month a year as interim trainers, during the time the full-time trainers were on holiday. Jeffrey was content to strictly adhere to his training duties according to Lancaster's manual, but Sandy always managed to break the rules while working at the Center to the extent that Lancaster had no choice but to discipline her.

www.ingramcontent.com/pod-product-compliance
Lightning Source LLC
Chambersburg PA
CBHW020334260626
47156CB00004B/1520